OPERATION FAKE RELATIONSHIP

JAY NORTHCOTE

ACKNOWLEDGEMENTS

Thank you to my editor Victoria Milne, for making my words better; to my alpha reader Phoebe for keeping me going and not letting me give up; to Darcey for the sensitivity read, and to my proof readers: Alex, Karen and Laura.
Finally, last but never least—thank you to all my readers for supporting me and reminding me on a daily basis why I write.

COPYRIGHT

ONE

November

NICK STIRRED the sizzling pan and moved his body to the music that was pouring out of the kitchen speaker.

"It won't be much longer. Can you pass me another beer?" He glanced over his shoulder at his long-time friend and flatmate, Jackson. "Hey. Were you staring at my arse?"

"Hard not to when you're waving it in my direction." Jackson's tone was casual but he turned away quickly.

Busted. Nick reckoned his cheeks must be burning. "Good to know I've still got it." Nick grinned.

Jackson didn't respond to that. With his back to Nick, he got two beers out of the fridge and opened them, before passing one to Nick.

"Thanks." Nick went back to his stirring and dancing. He couldn't keep still when he was playing dance music. The track by Sash! poured through him, lighting up his muscles with the memory of all the nights he'd spent shaking his arse on a podium to pay his way through art college.

The music stopped abruptly, cut off by Nick's ringtone heralding an incoming call. "Bollocks." He stopped mid hip wiggle to glance at the screen. "Ugh. It's my mother."

"You wanna take it?" Jackson asked. "I can stir."

Curious as to why she'd be calling him, Nick picked up his phone. "Yeah. I'll get it over with. At least I have a legit excuse to keep the conversation short." He answered the call. "Hi," he said, tone carefully light despite the frisson of anxiety that ramped up his heart rate. What the hell did she want? She hardly ever called. Most of their communication was via the occasional email—which was how Nick liked it. He couldn't help wondering if this was something bad.

"Nick. Hello. It's me... Mum."

The sound of her voice alone was enough to make Nick's tension levels rise even more. His shoulders tightened and all the loose fluidity of his body from moments before vanished like water turning into ice.

"Hi, Mum." It felt odd calling her that, lending an ease and intimacy to their relationship that he'd lost a long time ago. He never referred to her as his mum when she occasionally came up in conversation with friends—or more often with his counsellor. She was always his mother then. "How are you?" He tried to sound a little more friendly than he felt as guilt and resentment tugged him in two directions.

"I'm fine," she said brightly. "How about you?"

"I'm good."

There was an awkward silence. They didn't talk often

enough to know much about each other's day-to-day lives so there were no threads to pick up, and Nick had no desire to attempt polite conversation.

"Did you want something?" he asked. "Only I'm in the middle of cooking—"

"Yes, I did actually." There was a pause as she sucked in a breath. "Nick... I'm calling to ask if you'd come home for Christmas this year."

It was Nick's turn to pause. Fighting the instinctive reaction to refuse immediately, he took a slow breath, gathering his thoughts.

Jackson gave him a questioning look. "You okay?" he mouthed.

Nick shrugged and then nodded to reassure him. Before he could decide how to respond, his mother continued.

"Please, Nick?" Her voice was soft with a rare edge of vulnerability. "I know you find family gatherings difficult, and I know you prefer to stay away. But Maria and Adrian are coming with Seth, and Pete's agreed to come this year instead of going snowboarding." Snowboarding? Since when was his brother into snowboarding? Nick was even more out of touch than he'd realised. "It's going to be Seth's first Christmas, and I know Maria would love both his uncles to be there for it. It's important to her."

"Why isn't she asking me herself then?" Nick sounded like a petulant child, but his stomach was churning. His sister, Maria, was the only person in his family he had a strong connection with. They'd remained close despite everything, and since she and Adrian had moved to Scotland, he didn't see her nearly as often as he would have liked. Seth had been born almost a year ago, and Nick had only seen him twice. He'd love to spend time with Maria and his nephew at Christmas, but not if it meant he had to spend time with his father too. Maybe he could arrange to visit her for a few days afterwards instead.

"Because she knows it would put you on the spot, and she doesn't want to use her baby as leverage to guilt trip you into agreeing."

Nick gave a bark of surprised laughter at his mother's honesty. "So you're doing it instead?"

"Yes." Her voice was determined. "I'm not above emotional blackmail. Maria isn't the only one who wants her whole family together for Christmas. It's been too long, Nick. It's time you and your father worked things out."

"I don't want—"

"Nick! I know things were difficult in the past but he's changed; you'll see that for yourself if you give him a chance. He's stopped drinking, and he's sticking to it this time. It's been almost a year now. I know he wants a chance to fix things with you, but he's too proud to ask for it himself."

Or too much of a coward, Nick thought. Anger clenched hot and tight in his stomach.

Then, more softly, his mother added, "I miss you, Nick. Please come home."

"I'll think about it," he said. "I can't talk more now. I have to go. I'm cooking and it's nearly ready."

"Okay."

"Bye, Mum." He ended the call and sank into one of the kitchen chairs with a growl of frustration.

"What's going on?" Jackson turned from the cooker and

raised a sympathetic eyebrow. Their friendship went back far enough that he'd witnessed Nick's rift with his parents.

"She wants me to come home for Christmas." Nick sighed. "And so does Maria... although apparently she wasn't going to tell me that. But my mother had no qualms about playing the nephew's-first-Christmas card to try and persuade me."

"Are you going to do it?" Jackson frowned.

"I dunno. Is that chicken done now?" Nick was hungry, and he wanted time for his whirling thoughts to settle a little. "Can we talk about it later?"

"Sure, man. Whatever you need."

They ate in front of the TV. Jackson picked *Deadpool* to watch—a favourite for both of them—and Nick was glad it was something he'd seen before because he wasn't able to concentrate on it properly. His relaxing Friday night had been knocked off course and anxiety tugged at him, like a child trying to get his attention.

He glanced sideways as Jackson laughed at something on the screen, and the hard edges of his mood softened a little.

Nick was grateful to have such a good friend. Although it was good to have someone to talk to when he needed, it was worth even more to have someone who let him *not* talk until he was ready. Jackson's solid presence made him feel comforted and safe. Jackson always had his back. He'd wait until Nick was ready to spill his tangled thoughts, and he'd help him unravel them if necessary.

· · ·

ONCE THE FILM was over and the credits were playing, Nick turned to Jackson and said, "I think I want to do it."

"Yeah?" Jackson picked up the remote and turned the TV off.

"Yep. I reckon I can handle being under the same roof as him for a couple of nights. At least he's not drinking anymore."

"Are you sure?"

"No," Nick replied. "Not at all. But it's the least shitty option. I want to see my sister and her family, and Maria wants to see me. I don't want all of us to miss out on being together because of my father."

"I get it." Jackson nodded and then added, "But I hope you're going to break it to my mum, because she'll be gutted you're not coming for Christmas there."

"Yeah. I'll tell her." Jackson's mum had become a substitute for his own, and she treated Nick like one of the family. His heart sank at the thought of missing out on their noisy, chaotic brand of Christmas.

Was he mad to go back home? He'd be lost among people who were worse than strangers. At least with strangers you had no expectations. Whereas most of Nick's family relationships were tense and difficult.

He'd barely exchanged more than a few words with his father in years. Even at his gran's funeral Nick had offered his condolences politely and then avoided his father for the rest of the afternoon. Things with his mother were tricky too, with years of resentment and guilt stacked up on both sides. He and his younger brother Pete had never got along well either. Close in age, but not in any other way, they'd spent their childhood arguing and fighting. During adolescence they'd grown apart, too different to find any common ground.

His sister Maria was the only one he could consider a true ally—and her husband Adrian—but they were bound to be distracted by the responsibilities of parenthood. Nick couldn't expect too much from them.

"I wish you could come with me," he said wistfully. "I could use the moral support."

There was a silence, and Nick immediately regretted voicing his thoughts. It wasn't fair to ask Jackson to give up seeing his own family at Christmas, even if it was feasible.

"I would," Jackson said. "If you want me to." His gaze was steady and sure.

"But I can't just invite you home for Christmas. They'd think that was weird. I mean... they know we're close and usually spend Christmas together at yours. But that's different."

"Hmm. I guess."

"Unless...." Cogs started to turn in Nick's mind as a plan formed. "What if I tell them you're my boyfriend now? Then it wouldn't seem odd to ask if you can come with me, and they can hardly say no, can they?" With Jackson by his side, Nick knew he could face his father's habitual disapproval and hostility.

Jackson's eyes widened. "Um, no. But, Nick...."

"Yeah. I know. It's not fair to ask you to give up Christmas with your own family. Sorry, man. It was a stu—"

"That not what I was going to say."

"What then?"

Jackson scrubbed a hand through his hair as he looked

down for a moment before meeting Nick's eyes. Brow furrowed, he asked, "Wouldn't it be weird? Pretending to be like, you know. Together... a couple, acting like we're in love with each other?"

Nick stared at him. He loved Jackson like a brother, and he'd never thought about him any other way. But Jackson was undeniably attractive. Although they were used to living together, he supposed that sharing a room—and a bed—would be a little strange. Nick's heart beat faster as his imagination filled in those gaps. "Yeah. I guess it would be. You're right. Just forget about it. I can go on my own." He swallowed. "It'll be fine. I can cope with a couple of nights, right?"

Jackson's face softened. "Nick. It's okay. I'll come."

A surge of warmth filled Nick, making his breathing catch. Jackson had always been Nick's protector, right from the moment they'd met in the club all those years ago, when Jackson had pulled an over-enthusiastic admirer off him. "I would love it if you did," he admitted in a small voice. "But only if you're sure."

"I'm sure," Jackson replied firmly. "My mum won't mind. She sees me often enough, and she'll have her hands full anyway with the rest of the family there."

"What about the weirdness? Do you think you can manage to put up with pretending to be a couple while we're there?"

"I'll find a way." The corners of Jackson's mouth lifted and his dark eyes gleamed with mischief as he added, "As long as you don't eat too much cheese because that makes you fart like a dog, and I'm not sleeping with you if that happens."

Nick laughed. "Okay. Deal. No cheese bingeing. I promise."

"Cool. Let's do it." Jackson held out his large hand for Nick to high five. They grinned at each other as their palms touched.

NICK WAITED a couple of days before calling his mother. Partly to let her stew, and partly in case Jackson changed his mind.

When he was ready to make the call, he went in the living room to find Jackson who was sprawled on the sofa with the Xbox controller in his hands. Two burly wrestlers were laying into each other on the screen.

"I'm going to go and phone my mother in a minute," Nick said. "This is your last chance to back out."

Jackson paused his game and looked up. "Nah. I'm in. It might be quite fun. It'll be like being a spy, or a secret agent or something."

Nick grinned. "So, you're ready to accept this mission?"

"Yeah. Operation Fake Relationship. Let's do it." Grinning back, he gave Nick a thumbs up before returning to his game.

Nick sat on the other end of the sofa, Jackson's familiar bulk right there next to him a reassuring reminder that he wasn't in this alone. "Here goes."

"Good luck."

Nick took a deep breath before hitting Call. Heart pounding, he waited as her phone rang and rang before finally going to answerphone.

"Fuck's sake!"

"What's wrong?" Jackson shot him a quick glance.

"Why don't people keep their phones on them? I mean, what's the point of having a mobile phone if it's not with you. It's a mobile. The clue is in the name!" All geared up to speak to her, he didn't want to do this in a message. "Ugh. I'm going to have to use their landline, and bet my father picks up."

Fuck it. He selected that number and hit Call again before he could chicken out.

"Hello?" His father's voice was still so familiar.

It made something resonate deep inside Nick, evoking a strange push-pull of yearning and fury. He gripped his phone and clenched his other fist, digging his nails into his palm. "Hi. It's Nick," he said curtly. "Is my... is Mum there?" The word *Mum* caught in his throat.

After a short pause his father replied, "Yes, hold on." There was a rustle and then his voice was more distant and muffled as he called, "Sue! It's Nick for you."

More rustling, and a few seconds later his mother was there, saying brightly, "Hi, Nick. How are you?"

"Fine." Nick wasn't here for chitchat so he cut to the chase. "I've decided that I'll come for Christmas, just for a couple of nights though."

"Oh, darling! That's won—"

"But I'll be bringing someone with me. I assume that'll be okay?" He poked Jackson with his socked foot, grinning at him as he turned in Nick's direction.

"Someone? Who?"

"My partner." He upgraded Jackson instinctively. Boyfriend sounded too casual, too young. Nick wanted them to take this fake relationship seriously. Jackson raised his eyebrows.

"Partner?" The shock was evident in her voice. She was clearly getting more than she'd bargained for when she'd asked him to come back to the fold.

Silence followed, so Nick clarified. "Yes, partner. You know, my significant other, boyfriend, other half. Whatever you want to call him."

"Yes, yes. I get it. Sorry. I'm just surprised because your dad and I had no idea you had a... partner." She said the word as if it was unfamiliar. "Maria never mentioned you were in a relationship."

Shit. Nick hadn't planned for that. He'd have to call Maria and explain. He knew he could trust her to go along with the pretence, and she'd convince Adrian to do the same. "Well, why would she?" he asked breezily. "It's not her news to tell, and she doesn't like playing go-between."

"Yes. Of course." She sounded abashed. *Nice save.* Nick mentally patted himself on the back as she continued. "Well. That's nice, Nick. What's his name?"

"Jackson." He let his gaze settle on his friend, whose focus was back on his game.

"Jackson? Isn't that the chap you share a flat with? Maria's mentioned him."

"Yes, that's right."

"I thought you were just friends."

"We are. I mean...." Nick floundered for a second. "We were. But one thing led to another." He grimaced at Jackson, who was chuckling at Nick's conversational flailing.

"Well, of course he's welcome to join us for Christmas. It will be nice to meet him at last."

"Are you sure Dad's not going to have a problem with it —with us?"

"No, no," she replied a little too quickly. "He wants the family back together for Christmas too, so he'll be fine, love. Don't worry."

Given his father's dubious attitude to homosexuality in the past, Nick doubted his father would be very happy with the situation. But if he wanted Nick back for Christmas, he was going to have to put up with him having a boyfriend. Jackson was part of the package.

"Okay, great." Nick was starting to like the idea now it was unfolding in his imagination. What better way to stick two fingers up at his father than rocking up for Christmas with Jackson in tow, and subjecting him to lots of PDAs. "I'll see you in a few weeks then. Bye, Mum." Maybe he could get used to calling her that again by Christmas if he kept practising it in his head.

"Bye, darling."

As Nick set his phone down he was feeling quite chipper.

"Partner, huh?" Jackson raised his eyebrows. "Sounds intense."

"I didn't think 'boyfriend' lent enough gravitas. I want my parents to take our fake relationship seriously."

Jackson snorted. "Of course you do."

Nick turned his attention to the screen, watching while Jackson threw his virtual opponent to the mat. "Nice move. You wanna watch something on TV when you're done with this match?" he asked.

"Sure."

As Nick settled down to wait, it occurred to him that it

shouldn't be too hard faking that he and Jackson were together. After sharing a flat for over a year and being best friends for nearly a decade, they were already like an old married couple.

This was going to be easy.

TWO

December

JACKSON GAVE a deep sigh of impatience as he waited near the tills in John Lewis. The queues were ridiculous, and Nick had only just joined the end of the line. He didn't see why Nick couldn't have ordered stuff online like any sane person. Christmas was still over a week away, so there would have been enough time. The shops might have been pretty with their lashings of fake snow, glitter, and excessive amounts of fairy lights, but they were also rammed with other shoppers.

"It'll be fun," Nick had said. "And I hate ordering online. I'd rather see what I'm getting."

Damn Nick for being so persuasive.

Jackson had skipped his morning trip to the gym to help Nick lug his shopping around, and surrounded by crowds of people he was feeling increasingly antsy and impatient. Tension was building in his back and shoulders. Helping

Nick carry his bags to the car wasn't going to be enough to burn it off.

He caught a woman looking at him nervously and realised he was scowling. With his height and build, Jackson looked pretty intimidating when he was in a bad mood. He smoothed his features into something more neutral and got out his phone as a distraction. Maybe if he played some of his music loud enough, it would drown out the annoying Christmas carols pealing through the speakers.

With the holidays fast approaching, Jackson was increasingly anxious about how things were going to go over Christmas. But he didn't regret his decision to go home with Nick.

Nick needed his support. Going back to visit would put Nick right in the thick of everything he'd worked so hard to detach from. Even if his father had stopped drinking, that couldn't take away from all the times he'd hurt Nick in the past. Jackson knew the hurt had been emotional rather than physical, but that didn't make it any easier for Nick to return. Anger rose as Jackson remembered how hard it had been for Nick to walk away, to cut himself off from his family—especially from his mum, and from Maria who'd still lived at home then.

Yeah. This was a massive deal for Nick. Of course he didn't want to go back there alone.

With a rush of uncomfortable honesty, Jackson realised he wouldn't want Nick to face his parents alone either. He was glad Nick had asked him to come, even if it meant not seeing his own family at Christmas.

He stared across at the line of shoppers. Nick was easy

to spot because of his hair. The burnt orange of autumn leaves, it caught the light and made him stand out from the crowd. Jackson's heart swelled with warmth at the sight of him and beat a little faster as he thought about what was coming.

As though he could feel Jackson's gaze on him, Nick turned and shot an apologetic grimace in his direction, and then he got out his phone and typed something.

A text alert interrupted Jackson's music, and he got his phone out to see Nick's message: *Sorry it's taking so long. Coffee's on me later.*

I should hope so, Jackson sent back. Then quickly added: *and cake too?*

Of course :)

Jackson looked across, hoping to see Nick's smile for real. He wasn't disappointed. He smiled back, heart thumping treacherously again as he wondered exactly what being Nick's pretend partner was going to involve.

Whatever. Your crush on him was over years ago, he told himself sternly. *He's your friend, and that's enough.*

THE NIGHT BEFORE CHRISTMAS EVE—WHEN they were due to travel to Nick's parents' place—they were sitting on the sofa watching *Bad Santa,* and drinking eggnog while they ate their way through a box of mince pies.

"How are you feeling about tomorrow?" Jackson asked.

"Okay... ish? I dunno. I've been trying not to think about it too much." Nick shrugged.

"Oh, sorry."

"Nah, it's all right. You know me. I prefer not to worry

about things until they happen." He rubbed at his shoulder and tilted his head to the side.

"Your neck hurting again?"

"A bit. I probably spent too long at my laptop finishing up that project last night."

"Do you want me to give you a shoulder rub?"

"Oh, would you? That would be awesome." Nick was already moving to sit between Jackson's feet on the floor. He tugged his jumper and T-shirt off as one and settled back between Jackson's knees.

"Pass the oil."

There was coconut oil on the coffee table, because this wasn't an unusual occurrence. Nick always seemed to have tight muscles in his neck and shoulders, so Jackson often gave him a massage in front of the TV. Sometimes Nick would return the favour if Jackson was sore from the gym.

As Jackson scooped a little oil into his palm, he wondered whether it was weird that they did this. There was an intimacy to it that seemed a lot for people who were platonic, even for two gay guys. Not that there was anything sexual about giving someone a massage per se, but the frequency of it, the easy routine they'd fallen into, was probably unusual.

It felt like the sort of thing a couple would do.

He smoothed the oil into Nick's shoulders, kneading the tense muscles and feeling them begin to soften as Nick gave a groan of appreciation.

"Hey, enough with the sex noises, man. We've talked about this," Jackson teased.

Nick's answer was an even louder groan, obviously exaggerated.

Jackson rolled his eyes even though Nick couldn't see him. "Idiot."

"I can't help it. You're too good at this."

"That's what all the guys say."

Nick chuckled. "All what guys? You're as much of a monk as I am."

It was true. Since splitting up with Tomas last year, Jackson hadn't made any attempts to find a new partner, or even hook up. After being in a long-term relationship, returning to casual dating and one-night stands held little appeal. His heart had been too bruised to face the inevitable rejections and uncertainty. He kept hoping he might meet someone more organically but hadn't had any luck yet.

Jackson carried on massaging Nick's shoulders, enjoying the sensation of smooth skin and lean muscle. Half-watching the movie again, his mind wandered. What would Nick's parents be like? And what would they make of him?

"Do your parents know I'm black?" he asked.

"No." Nick turned, surprised. "I don't think so. Unless Maria mentioned that, but why would she? Do you want me to tell them?"

"Nah. I just wondered. Never mind. It's not important."

"If they have an issue with it they can fuck right off." Nick's muscles tightened under Jackson's hands. "But I'm sure they won't. They have their faults but racism isn't one of them."

"Right." Although Jackson was the child of a white mother and British Caribbean father, he'd been raised in a predominantly white, middle-class area, so he was familiar with the subtle racism that could lurk behind polite smiles and attempts at political correctness. "Stop tensing." Jackson patted Nick's shoulders. "You'll undo all my good work."

"Well stop talking about my parents, then. You know that always stresses me out!"

Jackson chuckled. "Yeah. Sorry."

AS JACKSON LAY under the covers that night, his hand strayed to his dick as it often did as he was getting ready to sleep. He stroked himself idly as his mind drifted, wondering what the next few days were going to bring. Without his conscious permission his mind wandered down a path that led to him imagining how it would feel to have Nick lying in bed beside him. A surge of arousal rushed through him, but he shut it down instantly.

No. Not gonna go there.

When they first met, Jackson had got off thinking about Nick more times than he cared to remember. He'd admired him from afar at the club until the day he'd intervened when Nick had been getting hassled by some drunken lech. After that, they'd become friends, and Jackson had always wanted to ask him out but had never found the right moment. Nick was always involved with some bloke or other, and his boyfriends were always older and more sophisticated than Jackson, and they invariably treated Nick like shit. Eventually Jackson had given up on anything other than friendship and had allowed himself to fall for Tomas instead.

Jackson's feelings for Nick were so far in the past, it felt wrong fantasising about him now, almost as if he was thinking about his brother. He pulled his hand out of his boxers and rolled onto his side, hands tucked safely under his pillow where they couldn't touch his dick.

But Nick isn't your brother. A treacherous little voice argued, trying to give him permission.

Jackson pressed his face into the pillow and groaned. If he was going to get through Christmas without making things awkward, he was going to need to get better at training his brain—and his body—to behave.

He'd realised long ago that he wasn't Nick's type. He was too nice. Nick was attracted to narcissistic wankers, and watching the pattern repeat over and over had been almost too much to bear. When things inevitably went to shit, Jackson was always there to pick up the pieces of Nick's broken heart. Thank fuck it had finally stopped a couple of years ago when Nick had started having counselling. Since then, he'd remained single—and celibate—and seemed happier for it.

"ARE YOU OKAY?" Jackson glanced at Nick.

"Yes!" Nick frowned at the road ahead and tightened his grip on the wheel. "Well, actually *no*. I'm not, but I can deal with it. And you asking me every ten minutes isn't helping matters."

"Right." Jackson clenched his hands into fists, trying to resist the urge to snap back.

Nick wasn't the only one who was nervous. Jackson wasn't looking forward to the impending introductions either, but he didn't think bringing that up would help. "I'll try and stop asking."

At least he'd finally got an honest answer. Nick had been wound tight all day, stressing out over packing and worrying about what time to leave. Then he'd insisted on driving even though Jackson had offered. The traffic had been predictably awful getting out of London with hordes of Christmas Eve travellers on their way out of the capital, and Nick had spent most of the three-hour trip yelling at other road users.

Nick sighed. "Sorry, mate. I'm just... well, you know. My head's all over the place. But I shouldn't be taking it out on you." He flashed Jackson a sheepish smile.

"Yeah, you shouldn't. But I'll let you off."

"We're nearly there now. We come off at the next junction and then it's not far. I'll probably feel better once we've got the first meeting over with."

They were deliberately arriving late in the day so they'd be the last of the family to arrive. Nick was trying to minimise the time he had to spend with his parents.

"So... um. How are we going to play this whole pretending to be partners thing?" Jackson asked. "Do we actually need to do anything much different to normal? I'm guessing not really, apart from sharing a room of course...."

"Oh, I definitely want to be obvious about it!" Nick said. "My father made me feel shitty about my sexuality from the moment I realised I was different. I internalised so much homophobic crap from him because of comments he'd make about stuff on TV or in the news. He stopped that after I came out, but it was too late. I knew what he thought already. So, I want to flaunt my sexuality now. I want to show him that I'm not ashamed of who I am."

"Okaaaaay." What on earth had Jackson let himself in for? "What sort of thing did you have in mind?"

Nick must have heard the trepidation in his tone because he chuckled. "Don't worry. I'm not planning on grabbing your dick in front of him or anything. I'm just talking casual touches, hand holding, putting an arm around you on the sofa, maybe a kiss on the cheek here and there—and a snog under the mistletoe, of course."

Jackson managed a nervous laugh in response. "Oh right. Yeah. Course." His brain was still unhelpfully locked onto the idea of Nick grabbing his dick.

"Come on, surely snogging me isn't that terrible a prospect? I've been told I'm a great kisser, and I have good oral hygiene."

"I'm sure I'll cope." Jackson managed to keep his tone light, but his heart was thumping hard.

Twenty minutes later it was beating even faster as Nick turned off a narrow country lane onto a track lined with tall evergreen hedges, saying, "Here we are."

The track opened out onto a gravel drive in front of a building that looked as if it might once have been a farmhouse. The winter afternoon sunshine lent extra warmth to the limestone walls. It was beautiful, and so was the rambling garden that surrounded it.

Jackson stared in amazement. "Wow. You never let on your home was as fancy as this."

"It's not my home," Nick said flatly.

"Okay, but you know what I mean. Is this where they lived when you were growing up?"

"Yeah."

"It's pretty impressive."

Nick shrugged as he drew to a halt in front of the house. "I suppose. I just took it for granted when I was a kid. Right. You ready for this?"

"Not really. You?"

That earned him a chuckle. "Nope. But let's get it over with."

They got out of the car. Jackson went to open the boot, but Nick said, "Leave the cases for now. Come on."

As they approached the front door together, Nick took Jackson's hand. "Is this okay?" he asked quietly.

"Yeah." Jackson hoped his palm wasn't too sweaty with nerves. "It's fine."

THREE

Nick's stomach was churning with anxiety as he rang the doorbell. With every cell in his body screaming for him to run in the opposite direction, only the warm reassurance of Jackson's hand holding his in a steady grip stopped him from bolting.

"I'm so glad you're here," he muttered.

Jackson squeezed his hand more tightly.

A few more painful seconds ticked past, and then finally the door opened to reveal Maria beaming at them.

"Nick, Jackson! The happy couple." She winked meaningfully at them before sweeping them both into a hug and kissing their cheeks. "Seriously though, Nick," she whispered. "I can't believe you're doing this, but I'm so glad you're here. It will be awesome to spend Christmas with you—both of you." She smiled at Jackson as she released them.

"Yeah, well. I reckoned it was about time." Nick managed a grin. It was hard not to be cheered by Maria's obvious joy at their presence.

"Come through to the living room, Mum and Dad are in there." She turned to lead the way.

Nick shut the front door and followed with Jackson by his side. An army of butterflies was rampaging in his gut as he braced himself to face his father. He grabbed Jackson's hand again.

When they entered the room, Nick scanned it like a grazing animal seeking out predators, and a surge of adrenaline rushed through him as he met his father's cool grey gaze for a split second, before his father switched his attention to Jackson. Nick felt savage satisfaction as his father's mask of impassivity slipped, eyes widening as he studied Jackson. His gaze dropped briefly to their joined hands before he stood to greet them.

"Nicky, darling! It's so lovely to see you." His mother swooped in, and he had to let go of Jackson's hand to give her a hug and a kiss on the cheek.

"Hello. It's good to see you too," he said politely. Maybe it would be good. It was too soon to tell.

He'd missed her when he'd first started distancing himself from his father, but the loss of their relationship had been collateral damage. Her loyalty to Nick's father had made it impossible. They'd kept up communication, but had rarely spent any time together in person. All their meetings had been at weddings, funerals, or other large social gatherings, so there had been little opportunity for any genuine connection.

He disentangled himself gently. "Jackson, this is my mother. Mum, meet Jackson."

"Jackson, welcome." Her smile was unnaturally bright and her voice smooth with a veneer of careful politeness as she offered Jackson her hand. "We've heard about you. But it's lovely to meet you at last."

"You too, Mrs Carling." Jackson shook her hand.

"Sue, please. No need to stand on ceremony." She gave a nervous laugh.

"Sue." His deep voice was warm and sure. Nick envied his confidence and wondered what was going on beneath the surface. He felt a flash of guilt as he realised he'd been so wrapped up in his own angst all day, he hadn't even asked Jackson how he was feeling. All he'd done was snap at him when he'd tried to be supportive.

Nick turned to his father, who extended his hand and gave an awkward nod.

"Nick," he said gruffly.

Nick shook his hand, deliberately using a firm grip. "Dad." The word nearly stuck in his throat, but he'd never called him Father growing up, and to do so now would sound passive–aggressive and weird.

His father turned to Jackson next, sticking his hand out again. "Jackson. Welcome."

"Hi, Mr Carling. Thank you," Jackson said. Nick felt a twist of smug satisfaction as he noticed how Jackson's hand dwarfed his father's.

Nick's mother cleared her throat rather pointedly.

"You can call me Reg." Nick's father released Jackson's hand and stepped back. "How was your journey? Was the traffic bad?"

"Hellish," Nick said, trying not to grin with relief. Discussions about traffic and the weather were the grease that kept all British social interactions from getting too sticky. "But at least we were expecting it. It's inevitable on Christmas Eve isn't it?"

His father made a grunt of agreement.

"Yes, absolutely." His mother nodded. "It's always dire."

"Where's everyone else?" Nick looked around.

"Adrian went running with Pete," Maria explained. "And Seth's asleep, but I'm going to get him up soon if he doesn't wake, otherwise he won't sleep tonight."

"Do you want to bring your bags in from the car?" his mother asked. "I'll warm up some mince pies and put the kettle on while you do that. Would you like tea or coffee?"

"Tea please," Nick replied.

"Yes, tea for me too," Jackson said.

"Where are we sleeping?" Nick asked. The "we" gave him another little thrill. It felt good facing his parents as one half of a gay couple, even if it wasn't a real relationship.

"In your old room," his mother replied without batting an eyelid. "But don't worry, there's a double bed in there now."

"Glad to hear it. I think we'd struggle to share a single, wouldn't we, babe?" Nick nudged Jackson, who grinned.

"Yeah. I can barely fit in a single bed on my own."

Nick couldn't resist a glance at his father, who was looking as if he'd sucked on a lemon. "Right. Let's go and get our stuff," he said breezily.

"Babe," Jackson said as soon as they were out by the car. "Really?"

"It just came out. I was ad-libbing." It had felt strangely natural, but Nick wasn't going to admit it.

Jackson reached for his case, lifting it effortlessly. "So

what pet name am I gonna call you then? Sweetie? Sugarplum?"

Nick chuckled. "I'll leave that up to you to decide." He grabbed his case and hauled it out of the car. There was nothing left to carry because Jackson already had the two bags containing gifts and bottles of wine in his free hand. "Want me to take one of those?"

"Nah, I'm good."

"Might as well put all those muscles to good use."

"Indeed. Use it or lose it." Jackson grinned.

Nick studied him for a moment. Jackson's body was the perfect inverted triangle of masculinity with broad shoulders tapering to a slim waist and hips, but his arse and thighs filled out his jeans perfectly.

Damn.

Nick mostly forgot how attractive his best mate was, because he'd known him for so long that he took it for granted. But Jackson really was a fine-looking man.

"What?" Jackson quirked an eyebrow, expression curious.

Nick grinned. "I was just thinking I've done all right for myself ending up with you as a partner. You're pretty hot."

Jackson's eyes widened and a strange tension buzzed between them for a second or two, until Jackson seemed to recover from his surprise. "Well thanks, honey," he said casually. "You're not so bad yourself."

"Honey?"

"Yes. Deal with it. Come on. Let's get these inside," Jackson said. "I'm more than ready for that cup of tea and a mince pie."

When they reached the top floor landing, Nick opened the door to his old bedroom and was surprised to find it wasn't that different to how he remembered it. The walls had obviously been repainted since he'd ruined them with Blu-Tack and band posters, but they'd been done in a very similar shade of greyish-blue to what had been there before. The carpet and curtains were the same, and so was the furniture —aside from the double bed that now dominated the space. The spines of the books on the shelves were familiar, titles he'd read as a child, and even some old school textbooks.

Some of his old tat had obviously been thrown out, or boxed up for storage, so it wasn't quite an untouched shrine awaiting his return. But it also wasn't the soulless spare room he'd been expecting. Although his cherished band posters were gone, they'd been replaced with some rather nice paintings. Nick paused to admire one that depicted a thatched cottage he recognised from a nearby village. They must have been done by a local artist.

"Which side of the bed do you want?" Jackson asked. "Door or window?"

"Window." Nick put his case down on the foot of the bed and went to look out at the view he remembered so well from childhood.

The garden hadn't changed much either, with the same flower beds and mature shrubs around the edge of the lawn. The silver birch at the bottom of the garden was much taller now; it had almost caught up with the trees in the wood beyond the fence.

"That seemed to go okay." Jackson's voice pulled Nick back from memories of summer days spent making mud pies in the flower beds with his siblings, or of chasing them around the garden with the hose.

"Hmm?"

"Meeting your folks. The reunion. It went pretty smoothly."

"I guess."

Nobody had yelled at anyone. Braced for drama, Nick had found the calm almost disconcerting. In some ways it had felt more like meeting distant acquaintances rather than the people who had raised him.

Nick sat on the edge of the bed and bounced. "This feels comfy. Much better than my old bed." He bounced harder, making the bed frame creak. "It's a bit squeaky though."

"Stop it!" Jackson said. "That probably sounds really dodgy from below."

Nick grinned. "Lucky we're two floors up from the living room then. Do you reckon they'd think we're at it the minute we're behind a closed door?" Then he gave a snort and added, "Actually, yeah. My father probably would. I bet he thinks us gays are all sex-crazed and constantly at it like rabbits. I reckon that's part of why he's a homophobe— he's jealous that he's missing out on all the orgies."

Jackson laughed. "You reckon?"

"That's one of my theories."

"Well stop bouncing, and start unpacking. I'm hungry."

It didn't take long for them to unpack their cases.

"What shall we do with those?" Jackson gestured to the other bags.

"We might as well take them back down. Put the presents under the tree and give Mum the wine and chocolates." He had asked his mother whether he should bring wine or something non-alcoholic instead. Much to his relief she'd said wine was okay. Nick hadn't fancied doing Christmas without a bit of booze to smooth the raw edges.

They went downstairs.

"I think someone's in the kitchen. This way." Nick followed the sound of clattering. "Hi, Mum. We brought some bottles of wine and chocolates. Shall I leave them on the counter?"

"Yes. Thanks, darling." She looked across from where she was getting out some plates. "They look lovely."

"Do you need a hand with anything?" Jackson asked.

"No, but thanks for the offer. You two go on through to the living room. I think Maria's just getting Seth up."

They found Nick's father alone, sitting in his armchair doing the crossword. He glanced up as they came in and gave them a brief nod.

"Shall I put the presents under the tree?" Nick asked. Although the tree was set up in the usual place in the bay window, festooned with baubles, tinsel, and fairy lights, the floor beneath it was surprisingly bare for Christmas Eve.

"Um. Yes, I suppose so," his father said. "But it's maybe best to leave them in the bag for now. Maria's been having trouble keeping Seth away from the tree as it is."

"Wow. So he's crawling then?" Nick tucked the bag away in the corner behind the tree.

"He certainly is. And he's into everything." His face softened, splitting into an indulgent smile Nick didn't recognise as he looked past Nick at the door. "Speaking of which... here he is, the little monkey."

Nick turned to see Maria coming in with a sleepy-looking Seth on her hip. "I had to wake him up or I think he'd have slept on till dinner time," she said as the baby studied the new arrivals suspiciously.

"Will he remember me?" Nick asked. It had been about three months since he'd seen them.

"Probably not. But he warms up to new people pretty quickly. Sit down. He'll chill out faster if you're not looming over him."

Nick and Jackson sat on one of the sofas, while Maria sat on the other with Seth on her knee. He stared at Nick, and then Jackson, studying them both carefully before he seemed to decide they weren't a threat, and he started to wriggle to get down.

"Okay, go on, then." Maria put him on the carpet by her feet. He sat there for a moment, before rocking forwards onto his hands and knees and crawling towards Jackson.

"Wow! Look at him go," Nick said.

"Bit of a change since you saw him last?" Maria asked.

"Totally." Nick stared in amazement as Seth hauled himself up on the legs of Jackson's jeans till he was standing on wobbly legs, swaying like a drunk and grinning in delight.

"Hey there, buddy." Jackson smiled, and the sight of him grinning at the baby made something warm unfurl in Nick's stomach.

"I can't believe he can stand up now. That's mad."

"I know!" Maria smiled. "It really is. I don't think he's far off taking his first steps."

"Hey, Seth," Nick said. "Look at you!" He held out a hand to Seth, who sidled towards him and then grabbed

Nick's fingers in his chubby hand before losing interest, plopping down on his bottom, and then crawling off at high speed towards the Christmas tree.

Maria intercepted him, scooping him up and ignoring his squawk of protest. "Here, Sethie. Let's get some of your toys out."

"I bet he's hard work now he's moving," Jackson said. "I remember the crawling was a game-changer with my niece."

"God, yes. He's running us ragged." Maria chuckled. "I'm so grateful he has at least one long nap every day otherwise I'd be a wreck. "Look, Seth, let's play with your ball, not the tree." She sat on the floor and rolled a soft ball towards Seth. "Roll it back to Mummy. That's it."

Nick's mother came in, saying, "Right. The mince pies are ready. Can someone come and help carry a tray?"

Jackson got to his feet immediately. "Of course."

That earned him a smile. "Thank you, Jackson."

Nick felt a flush of pride. Jackson was being a perfect fake boyfriend. His mother definitely seemed to approve so far.

Jackson returned bearing a tray laden with plates, cups, saucers, a teapot, a jug of milk, and a sugar bowl. No wonder Nick's mother hadn't wanted to carry it. "Just pop them down over here. That's perfect," his mother said. Jackson placed the tray carefully on a low cupboard behind the sofa. "Seth can't reach up here so they'll be safe." She put down the large plate of mince pies next to the tray and started laying out cups and saucers.

The sound of the front door heralded the return of the runners.

"Your timing couldn't be more perfect!" Maria said as Adrian and Pete came in, pink-cheeked and breathless.

"Mince pies? Wicked." Pete's eyes lit up, and then he noticed Nick. "Hey, bro. Good to see you."

"You too." Nick stood as he made his way over.

They hugged briefly.

"How are you?" Pete asked.

"I'm good. You?"

"Yeah, not so bad." Pete turned and looked at Jackson with interest. "You must be Jackson, right? Good to meet you, man."

"You too." As they shook, Nick noticed Pete drawing himself up to his full height and squaring his shoulders. He wondered whether he was aware he was doing it. Pete was a couple of inches taller than Nick—which had been a huge source of irritation for Nick when his younger brother had overtaken him—but Pete still had to look up to Jackson. Nick bit back a satisfied smile.

Adrian approached next. "Hi." He gave Nick a hug first and then Jackson. "It's really great to see you both again."

"You've met Jackson before?" Pete asked.

"Yeah, Maria and I stayed with them in the summer."

"Oh, right. So how come I was the last to know about this big romance?" Pete gestured from Nick to Jackson. "Nobody tells me anything!"

"Maria knew because she actually keeps in touch," Nick said dryly. "I think the last time I heard anything from you was a birthday card, and that arrived a week after my birthday."

"Yeah, okay. Fair enough." Pete grinned. He might have

been an annoying git sometimes, but he was good-natured. "I guess that's me put in my place."

"We didn't know anything either." Nick's father's tone cut through the light-hearted teasing like a cold draught. "So you weren't the only one in the dark."

There was an awkward silence.

"Right, tea and mince pies anyone?" Nick's mother said brightly. "Let's eat them before they get cold."

The palaver of distributing tea and mince pies to everyone, while also keeping Seth busy so he didn't grab anyone's tea, was a welcome distraction. By the time Nick was on his second mince pie the tension in the room had mostly dissolved. Pete was telling him all about his new job, and Jackson was chatting with Adrian. Seth was hanging onto Maria's legs, eyeing her mince pie and ignoring the rice cake he'd been given to eat instead.

Nick found himself zoning out as Pete started telling him about the snowboarding trip he had planned for New Year. He glanced surreptitiously at Jackson, who seemed far more at home here than Nick did.

Irritation crept over him like toxic mist.

Why did I agree to come?

Sure it was nice to see Maria and her little family, but he could live without the rest of them. His gaze drifted to his father, who was doing his crossword again and not even attempting to make conversation with anyone. What was the fucking point in being here? He should never have come, and he should never have dragged Jackson along with him. Nick could visit Maria any time and not have to put up with feeling so uncomfortable.

Suddenly, unable to bear it anymore, he stood. "Excuse

me, Pete. But I need to stretch my legs before it gets dark, so I'm going to head out for a quick walk."

"Do you want company?" Jackson asked.

"If you like." Nick caught a flash of hurt surprise on Jackson's face and realised too late that his tone had been rather curt. He tried to fix it with a smile as he added, "It would be nice to show you around."

"Okay." Jackson returned his smile warily.

"Yeah, and I need to go and shower. I probably reek." Pete sniffed his armpit.

"Peter!" his mother said reprovingly.

OUTSIDE, the winter sun hung low in the sky and the temperature was dropping fast. Nick was glad they'd wrapped up warm. He breathed in the clear, crisp air and let it out in a sigh of relief.

"God, it's good to be outdoors."

"Yeah. It's beautiful." Jackson looked around. The afternoon was turning into evening and the golden light was already tinged with orange, promising a beautiful sunset. "Which way are we walking?"

"Through the back garden. There's a gate that leads into the woods."

They walked in silence for a while. Fallen leaves crunched under their feet, and birds sang in the branches above them, heralding the ending of the day.

"This isn't what I expected," Jackson said.

"What? My family?"

"Not your family so much as the place. I didn't realise

you'd grown up in such a rural setting. I'd always imagined it as more suburban, like where my mum lives."

"It's not that different really. The other side of the village is more like the estate where you grew up. My parents are lucky to live on the edge so they get the countryside. They were always worried this land behind the house would be sold to a developer, but it hasn't happened yet."

"How are you feeling now you're back?"

"I don't know." Nick didn't want to talk about it. He hadn't had time to assess it for himself yet. "It's too soon to tell. I'm just glad that you're here to keep me company." He shivered. "It would be shit to be here on my own."

Despite the civil veneer, he could already feel the pull of old family dynamics he'd been glad to escape from. Without Jackson as a buffer it would have been unbearable. Just one conversation with Pete bragging about his career and his expensive holidays had reminded Nick how competitive he'd been as a kid, and how Nick had always felt eclipsed by his younger brother who was smarter than him, sportier than him, *straighter* than him. His father had always approved of Pete's choices and never supported Nick's.

Fuck him. I don't need his approval.

He kicked a rotten piece of wood, sending it flying into a nearby tree.

Jackson didn't comment.

They emerged from the wood and climbed over a stile into a grassy field. A flock of sheep eyed them curiously, and then carried on grazing as they turned and followed the path along the edge of the field. Nick put a hand on Jackson's arm. "Let's stop for a minute."

Standing side by side, they admired the view. The sun would be setting soon, and the sky faded from blue overhead through shades of yellow and gold to pale orange at the horizon.

"There's not a single cloud," Jackson said. "Shame there's no snow forecast. I'd love a white Christmas."

"I'll settle for frosty." The last thing Nick wanted was snow, that might stop them escaping back to London as soon as Christmas was over. "It's going to be freezing tonight. Lucky I'll have you to keep me warm." Nick turned with a grin, hoping for a chuckle in return.

"Look!" Jackson pointed. "What's that? Are they birds?"

Nick followed his gaze to see a cloud of black specks moving together against the glow of the sky, twisting and turning as one like iron filings pulled by an invisible magnet. "Yes. They must be starlings. I remember seeing them do that when I was a kid."

"There must be hundreds of them. Wow, it's amazing how they move. How do they know which way to go?"

"I don't know."

The birds swooped higher, spreading out like smoke dissipating before gathering back together in a dense ball. Nick and Jackson watched in wonder as the starlings continued their complex dance for a few minutes, before finally settling into a copse of trees a few fields away.

"That was incredible." Jackson's eyes were bright with wonder. "I've never seen anything like that before."

Nick smiled. "I'm glad they put on a display for you."

"Me too."

There was a softness to Jackson's expression that made Nick feel as though one of the starlings had broken free from the flock and was flapping its wings inside him.

"Come on, I'm freezing," he said briskly. "Let's head on."

FOUR

Jackson's spirits had been lifted by the sight of the starlings, and his heart felt light as they continued their walk. The sun was a ball of fire, resting on the dark horizon.

When the path looped back into the woods, Nick paused. "Want to watch the sun set?"

"I thought you were cold?"

"I am. But it won't take long, and it'll be worth it. Come here. We can huddle like penguins." He reached for Jackson and wrapped his arm around his waist. Jackson put his arm around Nick's shoulder and pulled him closer. With the height difference, they fitted perfectly like this. "That's better."

They stood, watching as the sun inched its way lower and lower.

"Isn't this romantic?" Nick said, turning to Jackson with a smile. "It's a shame we're not really a couple, because this is the stuff soppy movies are made of. It's sadly wasted on us."

Jackson chuckled, hoping he sounded convincing, and

looked away quickly. "Yeah. Right. Look at the sun, you idiot, or you're going to miss it setting after making us stop and watch." Eye contact was too much when they were standing so close. It made him want to do something crazy, like tell Nick how beautiful he looked, or kiss him, or something.

They waited in silence until the last sliver of gold disappeared, and Nick pulled away.

"Come on, then. Let's head back."

It was only then that Jackson realised how dark it was, even more so as they followed the path into the woods. Hurrying along behind Nick, he tripped over an invisible obstacle. "Fuck!" Throwing his arms out, he managed to catch his balance. "Slow down."

Nick stopped and got out his phone to use as a torch. "That's better. Have you got yours too?"

"No. I left it charging when we came out."

"Give me your hand then."

Jackson hesitated a second before taking Nick's hand. They were both wearing gloves, and Jackson found himself wishing they weren't so he could have felt Nick's skin warm against his own.

With the light of Nick's torch they made their way carefully through the woods until Nick stopped by a huge tree. He left the path and circled around it, shining his torch at the base.

"What are you doing?"

"Just checking something." There was a scuffling sound and the light disappeared.

"Nick?" Jackson asked, alarmed.

"Hang on." Nick's voice was muffled and distant. Jackson

felt his way around the trunk. As his eyes adjusted he could just make out the trees around him, but there was no sign of Nick.

"Where the fuck did you go?" Jackson looked around wildly.

"I'm in the tree."

Jackson looked up, but there was no way Nick could have climbed it.

"Look down!"

A light flashed near his feet and Jackson noticed a hole in the trunk. At first glance it looked way too small for Nick to have crawled inside it. But when Jackson crouched down for a better look, he saw it was larger than he'd thought. "Come and see."

Against his better judgement, Jackson eased his head and one shoulder through the hole. "Bloody hell. I thought you'd been abducted by aliens for a minute there."

"Nope." Nick had climbed a little way up, his feet were straddling the inside of the hollow tree. "Wait there for a sec."

"I wasn't planning on going anywhere," he replied as Nick started scrambling higher. "Ugh." He jerked his head back as a few bits of tree dust landed on his face.

"Yes!" Nick's voice was triumphant. "It's just how I remembered. Come and join me."

"You're kidding, right? I'm never going to fit up there."

"Yes you will. It's more roomy than it looks."

Still unconvinced, Jackson's curiosity got the better of him. Sure enough, once he managed to wedge his shoulders through, the rest of him followed fairly easily. Inside, it was a tight fit, but he was able to stand and lift his arms. He felt around for a handhold. "How do I climb up? I can't see a fucking thing, Nick."

"Here you go." Blinding light flashed in his eyes, and he held up a hand to cover them.

"Not helping!"

"Sorry. But look down, not up. See, there's a couple of little footholds. Just brace your hands against the sides and work your way up. Then once you get higher there's stuff for your hands too.

"If I get stuck in here it's going to be really embarrassing. You know that, right? I wasn't planning on spending Christmas Eve having the fire brigade cutting me out of a tree."

Nick laughed. "You won't get stuck. Stop being such a wuss."

Fucking cheek. Jackson sighed and started to climb.

It was dark, disorienting, and claustrophobic. "Now I know how Father Christmas feels going up and down all those chimneys. Poor bastard."

Nick's laughter gave him the boost he needed to keep going. "That's it. Nearly there. It's worth the effort, I promise. Now reach up... a little higher... move your hand to the right. There you go!"

As Jackson finally hauled himself up to where Nick was, he could see how the tree trunk opened out to form something rather like the edge of a crater from which the branches grew. "Okay. This is pretty cool."

"Told you so." Nick shone his torch around, and Jackson noticed that someone had added to the tree's natural platform by nailing two layers around the edge.

Nick was sitting on the higher one and resting his feet on the lower.

"It looks like one of those things they have on boats. You know... the lookout point at the top of the mast."

"A crow's nest?"

"Yeah. One of those. Are these planks safe?"

"I think so." Nick gave the one he was sitting on a good thump. "They're not that old, and they were good quality wood when we put them up. We treated so they wouldn't rot."

"We?" Jackson moved cautiously, clambering to sit on a plank opposite Nick.

"Me, Pete, and our father." Nick's voice sounded younger than usual, more vulnerable, as he added, "He helped us build it when we were kids. Maria was still too little. We called it the Pirate Tree."

"Must have been fun."

"Yeah. It was." His expression was hard to read in the darkness, but the wistful tone tugged at Jackson's heart. "We had some good times, especially when we were little. I have a lot of happy memories if I look back far enough."

"When did it change?" Jackson asked softly. Nick rarely talked about his childhood, not with Jackson anyway. Maybe he talked about it to his counsellor. Jackson knew what had happened in later years and knew why Nick had cut contact. But once he'd made that decision he hadn't wanted to look back. Even with Maria, their childhood was off-limits as a topic of conversation.

"I don't remember exactly. Maybe when I was twelve or thirteen? I know I was at secondary school, and not having a great time there. Dad lost his job and was really stressed about that. He started drinking more, and then his new job made him even more stressed. His drinking got worse and so did his mood. He stopped laughing, and he never had any time for us—unless he was criticising us for having messy rooms, or having a go at me for not working hard enough, or taking the piss out of me for wanting to be in the school play instead of on the football team." The angry bitterness in Nick's voice didn't mask the pain that lurked beneath. "Nothing I did was ever right. He made me feel as if I was never good enough, and that was *before* he knew I was gay." He stopped and let out a huff of frustration. "Ugh. Sorry. I'm ranting."

"It's okay. I asked." Jackson wanted to move closer, maybe offer a hug. But it was dark, and he was afraid of missing his step and falling down the hole in the tree.

"Yeah. But it's probably not the best time to get myself worked up over all that stuff when I have to go back and smile politely at him over dinner later. It's stupid that I still care anyway. It's all in the past."

"That doesn't mean it doesn't count." Jackson ached to wrap Nick tight in his arms and tell him he was absolutely good enough. He was perfect exactly as he was.

"Fuck him. I don't care what he thinks." The childish defiance in Nick's tone didn't ring true. It was obvious that he did care, no matter how much he protested.

But Jackson pretended right along with him. "Yeah. Good on you."

GETTING DOWN from the tree was only marginally easier than climbing up, but Jackson emerged unscathed.

The last hint of blue twilight had faded from the sky now, so Nick took Jackson's hand again and used his torch to light their way.

"This is the path that takes us home," he said as they took a right turn. "It's not far now."

When they finally reached the gate, Nick put his phone away and let them into the garden. Warm light poured from windows at the back of the house and they could see both Nick's parents busy in the kitchen. Reg was right by the window, head down, washing dishes by the look of it.

"Give me your hand again," Nick said. "In case they see us coming."

Jackson was happy to oblige, and as a security light on the back of the house came on Reg glanced up. He looked over his shoulder and said something inaudible, and then Sue appeared at the window beside him, waving cheerfully.

Nick waved back, keeping hold of Jackson's hand.

They let themselves in through the back door, leaving their coats and boots in the utility room.

The kitchen was warm and smelt savoury and spicy. "What's cooking?" Nick asked as they entered the kitchen.

"Chilli con carne," Sue replied.

"And apple crumble for pudding," Maria added. She was sitting at the table with Seth who was in a highchair, his face smeared with yogurt, and a plastic spoon in one chubby hand. Maria glanced over their heads and shot them a mischievous grin. "Aw, look, Nick. You're under the mistletoe. You know the rules."

Jackson looked up to see a large bunch of mistletoe tied up with red ribbon hanging from a hook in the ceiling.

"Of course," Nick said smoothly. "Come here, babe." Amusement curved his lips as he stepped in close and tilted his face up expectantly. He waited, eyebrows raised as if in friendly challenge.

What else could Jackson do? He'd agreed to this pretence, so he could hardly leave Nick hanging. Up close, he could see flecks of grey in Nick's blue eyes that he'd never noticed before. He put his hands on Nick's shoulders and quickly ducked his head, intending to give Nick a brief kiss on the lips. But as soon as their lips met, Nick curled his hand around the nape of Jackson's neck and held him there with enough pressure that Jackson got the message loud and clear.

Not so fast! He could imagine exactly how Nick would sound if he was saying it out loud, stern with a touch of humour.

Jackson gave in, letting Nick take charge of the kiss as their mouths softened against each other's. It wasn't a snog exactly. There were no tongues involved. But it was definitely more than a peck on the lips. It made Jackson's heart surge in a sudden thrilling rush because it was so sweet and gentle and *loving*.

Except it wasn't.

This was just for show, and that knowledge caused a dull ache in Jackson's chest as he longed for the real thing.

When Nick finally released him, Jackson's heart was thumping as if he'd done fifty press-ups.

"Happy Christmas," Nick said softly.

"It's not Christmas yet," Jackson managed.

"Well, Happy Christmas Eve, then." Turning away, Nick addressed his nephew. "Hey, buddy. The food's supposed to go in your mouth, not all over your face."

Maria laughed. "Yeah, we're still working on that, aren't we, darling?" Seth stuck his free hand in the yogurt pot and shoved a handful of it into his mouth, as if to prove Nick wrong. Then he threw his spoon on the floor.

Jackson picked it up. "Shall I give it back to him, or do you want me to wash it first?"

"You can give it back to him. But he'll probably drop it again immediately."

Sure enough, the moment Jackson put the spoon on the highchair tray, Seth grabbed it and flung it to the floor again with a joyful shriek.

"Well if you don't want it, it can stay there," Maria said calmly. "I think you're finished anyway."

Seth craned to see the spoon on the floor. "Ba-ba-bah!" He pointed.

"No. You're done. Let's get you cleaned up and I'll see if I can get Daddy to play with you while I sort out this mess."

"Want us to take Seth for a bit?" Nick offered.

"Oh, yes. That would be awesome. I'm not sure if Adrian will be out of the shower yet."

"No problem. Seth can have some quality uncle time."

Maria got a cloth and wiped Seth's face and fingers, and then removed his bib, which looked like an impressionist painting. "Right, that's good enough till bath time." She unclipped him and scooped him out of his chair. "Off you go with Uncle Nick and Uncle Jackson." She passed him to Nick, shooting Jackson a quick grin and a wink.

Jackson's cheeks heated as he grinned back. It felt good being referred to as Seth's uncle. Way too good.

He followed Nick into the empty living room.

"Right, Seth." Nick plopped him down on the carpet and sat cross-legged next to him. "What are we going to do?"

Jackson sat on the floor too, and they watched as Seth crawled off towards the basket of toys. He pulled out a few random things until he found a soft toy. It looked like a rabbit, with big floppy ears, and buttons for eyes. Some parts of it were furry, others smooth fabric, others textured. Seth poked the button eyes, and then scrunched one of the ears in his hands. It made a crackling sound.

"What have you got there, buddy?" Nick asked. Seth held the toy out towards him, and Nick moved closer, reaching out a hand to scrunch the other ear.

"Guh." Seth looked at him expectantly.

Nick scrunched the ear again. "Cool. Nice rabbit." He took the rabbit from Seth and wiggled it in front of him, putting on a silly voice and saying, "Hello, Seth! How are you today?"

Clearly unimpressed, Seth grabbed the toy and crawled towards Jackson, rabbit clenched in one determined fist. When he reached Jackson he shoved the toy in his lap. "Guh."

"Your turn." Nick grinned.

"Thanks, dude." Jackson smiled. "What do you want me to do with it?"

"Guh-guh." Seth sat in front of Jackson. "Guh-guh-guh!" His tone implied that whatever he wanted, it was very important.

Jackson picked up the toy and squeezed it, making it give a loud squeak.

Seth's face split into a huge smile and he flapped his hands in excitement. "Guh!"

"Ah, that's it." When Jackson squeaked the toy again, Seth gave an excited squeal, whole body bouncing as he flapped again.

"How did you work that out?" Nick looked a little disgruntled.

"Prior knowledge." Jackson tapped his nose with a smug grin. "It's not my first time playing with baby toys, remember." He had two nieces and a nephew, and sometimes babysat for his sisters.

The squeaking only kept Seth's attention for a couple of minutes though, and soon he was on the move again, pulling more toys out of the box. None of them caught his interest for long. Eventually he gave up on the toys altogether and started climbing over Nick and Jackson instead, as they sat leaning against the sofa with their legs stretched out along the floor.

"Do you want to have kids one day?" Nick asked.

Blindsided, Jackson considered the question. It wasn't something he'd given much thought to, but the answer rose from his gut and came out decisive. "Yeah. I do. You?"

"Yes. Definitely." Nick picked up Seth and lay him on his back on the floor, tickling his belly till he giggled. "I want a family."

"Two point four children?" Jackson teased.

"The point four can be a dog. I want one of those too."

"That sounds pretty awesome." Jackson briefly allowed himself to imagine an alternative reality where he and Nick got married and adopted two adorable kids and an adorable dog.

"Doesn't it?"

Seth twisted away from Nick's grasp and pulled himself up on Jackson's arm. He stood there for a moment, suddenly still and frowning in concentration. Then his face turned red and he made a grunting sound.

An unmistakeable odour intruded, chasing away Jackson's rose-tinted daydreams.

Nick laughed. "Thanks for the reality check, Seth. I think it's time we gave you back to your parents."

FIVE

They'd finished the main course and were having a short pause while the crumble finished cooking.

Nick watched his father as he took a sip of his tonic water, and then smiled at something Adrian had said.

It was weird watching him drink tonic while the rest of them were having wine. Nick was begrudgingly impressed at his determination. Surely it couldn't have been easy for him to be around other people knocking back the booze when he'd had a drinking problem.

Outwardly he seemed fine though. A little quieter than Nick remembered perhaps, and listening more than he was talking. But he seemed perfectly relaxed, and nobody else was behaving any differently around him.

Nick glanced around the table. Pete was well on the way to sloshed, which was usual for him. Maria and Adrian were drinking a little, but not excessively, and Jackson was only on his second glass. His gaze settled on Jackson for a moment, and his stomach fluttered as he remembered the kiss under the mistletoe earlier. Nick had felt off-balance ever since, as though something had changed even though it hadn't. The kiss hadn't meant anything, it had only been to show off in front of his parents.

So why did it feel so intense? And why can't I stop thinking about it?

The oven timer went. "That's the crumble ready," his mother said. "Let me go and get it out."

"It's okay, darling. I'll go." Nick's father was already on his feet.

That was new too. In the past Nick remembered his father letting her do the brunt of the cooking, serving, and clearing up. Now he was much more involved, and quick to help without her asking.

"Okay, thank you." She leant back in her chair and took another sip of wine. She sounded a bit tipsy, but she wasn't much of a drinker normally so a sniff of the barmaid's apron was usually enough to get her giggly and flushed.

Nick picked up his glass and took another swig. He'd already drunk more than he should. He could feel it in the fog that filled his brain and the pounding at his temples. Sitting in this room with his family, Nick felt as if he'd been transported back in time. They might all be ten or more years older, and there were a few extra bodies in the room, but the past loomed over him every time he caught his father's eye. Thank fuck Jackson was between them as a buffer. With Pete sitting opposite him droning on to their father about his promotion opportunities, and pay rises, and the house he was hoping to buy, pressure was building inside Nick like steam with no escape valve. The fuzziness gifted to him by the alcohol coursing through his veins and

Jackson's calm presence beside him were the only things keeping him at the table.

So far he'd managed to avoid any conversation with his father, talking mainly to Maria who was on his other side. That suited him just fine.

But once the pudding had been served, Pete had his mouth full of crumble and he finally shut up for a moment.

Their father turned to Nick. "So, how's your business going, Nick?"

Nick's heart started beating double speed at being the focus of his father's attention. "Good, thanks."

"You're still doing the same thing?"

"Graphic design. Yes."

"There's money to be made in that then?" The hint of surprise in his voice sent a hot rush of blood surging through Nick, heating his ears and making his collar feel too tight. His father had never supported his educational choices, sneering at his decision to study art and design rather than more academic subjects. He gritted his teeth, willing himself not to snap. "You're managing to earn a decent living with it?"

Nick lost the battle. "No, I have to sell my arse on the street corner to pay the rent every month," he snapped. "Yes, of course I earn a decent living. I wouldn't keep doing it if I didn't!"

Jackson choked on his crumble, and Pete's jaw dropped, eyes wide.

During the silence that followed, Nick's father's face turned an interesting shade of purple, and his eyes flashed as he glared. Nick felt savage satisfaction at seeing his relaxed demeanour finally slip. This angry version was more familiar, and Nick was strangely glad he'd managed to provoke him. When his father finally spoke, his voice was icy. "I was just making conversation, Nick. There's no need to be so sensitive, and there was no call for rudeness."

Nick wasn't going to defend himself, and he certainly wasn't going to apologise. "Well you should ask better questions. And *I* was only making a joke, so perhaps you're the one who's being over-sensitive."

There was an awkward pause, and then Nick's mother launched in with, "Jackson, what do you do?"

"I teach P.E. in a secondary school," Jackson replied.

"Oh, that's nice," she said brightly. "Do you enjoy it?"

"Mostly. Some of my classes are pretty challenging, but overall it's okay."

"No wonder you look so fit."

"He's a gym rat as well," Nick said, putting a hand on Jackson's bicep and giving it a squeeze. "Which explains the guns. Teaching alone wouldn't be enough to keep him looking *this* hot." He grinned at Jackson, who gave him a slightly strained smile in return.

There was another uncomfortable silence. Nick didn't care. He was enjoying making his parents squirm. It felt like revenge for all the times he'd sat at this table feeling angry, hurt, frustrated, inferior. He released Jackson's arm and took another spoonful of crumble.

The conversation started up around him again as Maria began talking about returning to work after her maternity leave. Nick zoned out, eating methodically and ruminating on the past.

Jackson sat silently beside him. A flash of guilt spiked through Nick. This couldn't be fun for Jackson. He'd ditched his own infinitely happier family Christmas for one that was full of stress and unresolved conflict. Nick deliberately shit-stirring was only making it more unpleasant for everyone—including the people around the table he didn't have issues with. Jackson wasn't the only one who fell into that category. He glanced at Maria and caught her worried gaze, and he resolved to try to behave better for the rest of the evening.

AFTER DINNER, they got out Pictionary, which had always been a family tradition. Apparently nothing had changed since Nick's last Christmas Eve with them.

"How shall we decide the teams?" Pete asked.

"Why don't you go with Nick and Jackson, and Adrian and I will make a four with Mum and Dad," Maria suggested quickly.

Thankfully there were no arguments about that as they rearranged the seating to fit the chosen teams. Maybe everyone realised that drawing lots for their teammates could have ended badly.

"I'm always happy to be on the same team as the professional artist for this game." Pete grinned at Nick and clapped him roughly on the shoulder as he took the seat beside him.

"Yeah, you see. I have my uses," Nick replied. Pictionary had been the one time where anyone in his family had appreciated his talents. Pete and their mother were both equally crap at drawing, and although his father was decent, he couldn't sketch fast under pressure. "Unfortunately my other half isn't so gifted in the drawing department, though." He patted Jackson on the thigh. "So you win some, you lose some." Jackson's leg felt wonderfully muscular through his trousers, so Nick left his hand there a little longer than necessary.

Jackson wasn't actually that bad at drawing, and Adrian and Nick's mother were both fairly terrible. So Nick's team were in the lead as they were getting towards the end of the game. When they landed on the final All Play square it was Nick's turn to draw for his team, while his father was drawing for the others.

Nick looked at the card and gave a snort of amusement. *Vibrate. This should be interesting.* "Here you go." He handed the card to his father.

There was really only one easy way to draw it, so as soon as the time started Nick went in for the kill and drew a large dick shape on the page.

"Um... what the hell?" Pete said. "I didn't think we were playing rude Pictionary!"

Nick ignored him, scribbling wiggly lines around it.

"Vibrating!" Jackson said. Nick nodded, drawing more lines and jabbing the paper with his pencil insistently. "Vibe... vibrator... vibrate!"

"Yes!" Nick burst out. "Nice one." As Jackson grinned at him triumphantly, Nick leant in and kissed him quickly on the lips.

Jackson's eyes widened for a second, but then he schooled his features into a casual expression that suggested he was used to Nick kissing him randomly. "Thanks," he replied. "I do my best."

Nick let his gaze linger on Jackson's mouth, and his lips tingled with another echo of their less-fleeting kiss under the mistletoe earlier. He'd managed to put it out of his head during the game, and now he remembered it again he felt edgy and unsettled. Was Jackson still thinking about it too?

"Yeah, good work, lads." Pete gave them a thumbs up. "I was no help with that one."

"That was bloody impossible," Nick's father said. "How on earth did you draw that?" He peered at Nick's drawing and his eyes widened. "Oh. Of course."

"C'mon. How else could you draw it?" He looked at his father's effort to see that he'd drawn a guitar with someone's hand and a vibrating string. "Oh yeah. I see what you were going for. But my way was much easier." He grinned. "You didn't stand a chance."

"Apparently not." Nick thought he heard a hint of humour in his father's tone, but his face didn't give much away.

AFTER THE GAME they sat and watched TV for a while until Adrian started yawning and set the rest of them off.

"Come on, darling," he said to Maria. "We'd better head to bed. No doubt Seth will be awake at some ungodly hour."

"Surely he's too young to be excited about Christmas?" Pete frowned.

Maria laughed. "Yes of course he is. But he wakes around six a.m. every day, so I doubt tomorrow will be an exception."

"Ugh. Rather you than me."

"I'm heading to bed too," Nick's mother said. "Are you coming, love?"

"Yes." Nick's father stood, stretching as he yawned.

Left alone with Pete, Nick and Jackson now had a whole sofa to themselves, so Nick took the opportunity to put his feet up. He lay with his head in Jackson's lap. "Is this comfy for you?" He looked up.

"Yeah." Jackson smiled down at him. "It's fine."

Pete had the remote and was channel hopping. The rapidly changing images and sounds were doing Nick's head in. "For fuck's sake, Pete. Pick something and stick with it."

"Okay, okay." He settled on *Independence Day*, which had only just started, moved from the armchair he was in to the other sofa, and lay down to watch it.

Nick had seen the film so many times he didn't need to pay much attention to it, which was good, because Jackson started stroking his hair, making it impossible to concentrate on anything apart from the delicious sensation. His fingertips sent sparks flying from Nick's nerve endings through his body, igniting a strange tingling warmth in the pit of his stomach.

"Mmm."

"Shh!" Jackson tapped his scalp lightly. Nick looked up to meet his gaze, and Jackson mouthed the words. "No sex noises."

Nick grinned and mimed zipping his lips before turning towards the TV again. He closed his eyes and let his mind drift as Jackson combed through his hair with gentle fingers. The alcohol in his veins made his head feel fuzzy and his limbs heavy. He was just starting to doze off when the sound of loud snoring from the other sofa tugged him away from sleep.

"Jeez," he grumbled. "Fucking Pete."

Jackson chuckled. "Yeah, that is impressively loud."

"He's ruining my nap."

"Want to head up to bed?" Jackson asked, his fingers still raking slowly through Nick's hair. He said it so easily, as if they always went to bed together. For a moment, still caught in the liminal space between sleep and full wakefulness, Nick could almost imagine he'd slipped into an alternate reality where they actually were a couple.

"Yeah. Okay." He sat and rubbed his eyes and then got up and reclaimed the remote from where it rested on Pete's chest so he could turn off the TV. "Pete.... *Pete!*" He poked his unresponsive sibling.

"Hmph. Whassup?"

"We're going to bed. I suggest you do the same. But bags we get to use the bathroom first." Pete's room was also on the top floor, and they shared a bathroom.

"'Kay."

Nick didn't reckon Pete was going to be moving anywhere for a while. "Well. I tried." He shrugged at Jackson. "Knowing Pete, he'll stumble up to bed in the small hours." They turned the lamps off and went upstairs, leaving Pete in darkness.

"I'm dying for a pee." Nick went straight into the bathroom to take care of business and then brushed his teeth afterwards.

In the bedroom he found Jackson sitting on the edge of the bed. "What are you waiting for?" Nick said. "I left the door unlocked." In the bathroom in their flat they thought nothing of pissing in front of each other or knocking elbows over the sink while they brushed their teeth.

"Oh, right. I wasn't sure whether I should."

"Jackson. They all think we're a couple, so nobody would bat an eyelid."

"Yeah. Course." He stood. "But this way you get to warm the bed up before I get in. It's bloody freezing."

This house was a lot colder than their well-insulated flat. Plus Nick's father had always been really strict about turning the heating down low at night, so the temperature was dropping fast. Nick stripped to his boxers and put on a T-shirt before slipping under the chilly covers. Thankfully the duvet was thick, and the bed warmed up fast. By the time Jackson returned Nick was very cosy and starting to feel sleepy again.

He half opened his eyes, watching as Jackson undressed with his back to him. Muscles moved beneath Jackson's skin as he slid his shirt off his powerful shoulders. Then he pulled on a grey T-shirt before dropping his trousers to reveal his muscular thighs. As he turned back to the bed, Nick closed his eyes quickly even though the sight of Jackson had woken him up a little.

"You still awake?" Jackson asked as he climbed in, bringing a blast of cold air with him.

"Yeah," Nick said, tugging the duvet up around his ears.

The bed creaked as Jackson shifted around, getting comfortable. "Damn this bed's loud."

"It is isn't it?" Nick sat up and bounced experimentally. "I reckon something needs tightening." He bounced harder. "The headboard's bumping against the wall too." He carried on, creating a rhythmic squeak-bump-squeak-bump and chuckling. "That really will sound dodgy from the room below."

"Who's room is that?"

"My parents."

"Nick, stop it!"

"Why? They know we're a couple. We're both consenting adults."

"We're not a couple, and I'm not consenting. Stop it!" Jackson grabbed him and pulled him down to the mattress, throwing his arm across his chest to keep him there.

"What's your problem?" Nick snapped in a flash of anger.

"I have to face your parents in the morning, that's what."

"So? There's nothing wrong with us having sex—I mean, if we *were* having sex, which obviously we're not." Nick was suddenly very aware of the fact that Jackson was half on top of him, his weight pressing Nick into the bed. Heat washed over him, flushing his cheeks. He tried to twist away but Jackson was too strong for him. "Maria and Adrian have Seth as evidence that they fuck, how is that any different?"

"It is different, and you know it." Jackson's jaw was set in determination. "And it will be really fucking uncomfortable tomorrow if you carry on doing that."

"I don't care. I *want* them to feel uncomfortable. It's about bloody time my father was the one to feel like that. I spent enough of my life feeling small, and shitty, and disapproved of thanks to him." A surge of hurt and rage rose, filling his eyes with furious tears. "I don't owe him anything." His voice cracked.

Jackson's face softened. "I know, Nick. I'm not saying you do. But... just. Please stop. I don't want to have to make polite conversation with your father tomorrow over breakfast while he has an image in his head of us having sex. Even if we *were* together I wouldn't want everyone in the house knowing we'd been fucking the night before. That would be private, something between us, and it would be nobody else's business." His intense expression and the quiet, intimate tone of voice sent all the fight and anger out of Nick like the *whoosh* of a balloon deflating, leaving behind a small, secret thrill of possibility that prickled under his skin like electricity.

"Oh."

Jackson's arm was still over him, but instead of restraining him it was more of an embrace now, his body warm and heavy. "If I let you go, are you going to behave?"

Nick was tempted to say no if that meant Jackson would keep him like this for longer. "I suppose," he hedged.

"Nick?"

"Okay, yes. Yes. I'll behave." He gave a mock pout.

"Brat." Jackson chuckled as he rolled away.

"You can't call me a brat. I'm older than you!" Outraged, Nick propped himself up on one elbow as Jackson lay on his back, expression serene.

Eyes closed, Jackson replied. "Only by six months. And being a brat has nothing to do with your age and everything to do with your attitude." He paused and then opened his eyes to glance at Nick. "Can we go to sleep now?"

"Yeah." Nick turned off the bedside lamp and settled down on his side, facing Jackson in the darkness. "Jackson?"

"Mmm?"

"I'm sorry... about before. I might want to make my father squirm, but I didn't want to make you feel embarrassed too."

"Okay. Thanks."

Relieved, Nick shut his eyes against the darkness and tried to recapture his sleepiness of before. Although he was tired, his head was full of thoughts about the evening. As Jackson's breathing slowed, Nick's brain was still buzzing. "Jackson," he whispered again after a few minutes.

Jackson sighed. "What now?"

"I'm sorry for the thing at dinner too."

"What thing?"

"The gym rat and muscles thing."

"Treating me like a prize bull, you mean?"

It was Nick's turn to squirm. "Yes. That."

"It's okay. You're forgiven."

"Thanks." A little more tension seeped out of Nick's body. "You're the best. I'll try not to rock the boat so much tomorrow." He gave a huff of amusement as he realised what he'd said. "Or the bed."

"That would be good. Night, Nick."

"Night."

SIX

Jackson drifted into consciousness at some point in the night. Barely awake and confused in the almost impenetrable darkness, it took him a moment to work out where he was. The bed felt strange and smelt of different laundry detergent to the one he used. Then a snuffling noise next to his shoulder reminded him he wasn't alone.

Nick.

He rolled away gently, not wanting to disturb Nick by making the noisy bed creak. His back to Nick now, he tucked one arm under his pillow as he nestled his head. It had been a long time since Jackson had shared a bed with anyone. A spike of loneliness came with that thought, and he hugged his pillow a little more tightly.

As if Nick had sensed Jackson's longing for contact, he rolled too, shuffling closer with an unintelligible mumble until he was spooning Jackson with one arm draped around him.

Jackson tensed. *Is he going to wake up?*

But Nick's breathing settled back into the slow steady rhythm of sleep.

Fibre by fibre Jackson's muscles relaxed again, and he allowed himself to lean into the solid warmth of Nick behind him. Eventually his breathing fell in sync with Nick's and the gentle rise and fall washing through his body lulled him back into slumber.

NEXT TIME JACKSON WOKE, they'd somehow switched positions in their sleep. Nick was curled in front of him in a foetal position with Jackson curved around him, arm around his waist. With Nick's arse pressed tight against Jackson's crotch and Jackson's hand brushing Nick's happy trail, this was definitely more than Jackson had bargained for when he'd signed up for sharing a bed with his friend. As he registered the proximity of their bodies and the intimacy of the position, an extra rush of blood went south, transforming Jackson's lazy morning semi into a critical boner in a matter of seconds.

He tried to move away stealthily, but as soon as he moved, Nick stirred. "Mmm. Feels nice." He pulled Jackson's arm up and held it against his chest.

Jackson froze, wondering precisely what Nick was referring to. *The cuddling? It has to be the cuddling.* Hopefully his dick wasn't that obvious. He forced himself to think of the least sexy things he could imagine: puke, clogged toilets, mushy peas, phlegm.... That soon fixed his problem and he was able to relax again. It did feel nice. Holding Nick like this was so natural, he could almost imagine that they woke up like this every day.

"Good morning," he said, his breath ruffling Nick's hair. "Did you sleep okay?"

"Yeah. Really well. You?"

"Yes." Considering the strange bed and the fact that he wasn't used to having company at night, Jackson had slept very soundly. "Oh, and happy Christmas. I nearly forgot."

Nick chuckled. "Me too. Happy Christmas. What's the time?"

"Dunno." Jackson had taken his watch off to sleep.

Nick stretched to reach his phone from the bedside table. "Just after eight."

"What does Christmas Day look like for your family? What time do things happen?"

"Well, unless it's changed significantly since I was here last, they normally open presents around midday. Mum used to always make pancakes for breakfast. I'm not sure what time that would be though; I should have checked last night. Hang on, I'll text Maria. She'll know."

He picked up his phone again and typed something, and then said, "She's replying." A pause. "Breakfast's at nine apparently."

"Cool. I wouldn't mind a shower before breakfast."

"Same. You can go first if you want," Nick said. "I'm feeling lazy, and I can't imagine Pete will be any competition for an early shower given the state of him last night."

Jackson snorted. "You're always feeling lazy." Nick wasn't known for his get-up-and-go in the morning. He almost always slept through his alarm. Although Nick worked from home, he often had client meetings or calls scheduled. After he'd missed a particularly important one that had cost him business, Jackson had taken to checking on him before he went to work, bringing him coffee, and kicking him out of bed if necessary.

"Yeah, I'm not going to argue with that." Nick rolled onto his back and stretched like a satisfied cat. He grinned, and Jackson's heart did a dangerous little flip. Even with his eyes puffy from sleep and his hair flat on one side and sticking up crazily on the other, Nick was gorgeous.

Jackson's gaze settled on Nick's lips for a moment and his mind shot back to Nick kissing him under the mistletoe. He wondered if that might happen again today, and he couldn't decide whether it would be wonderful or terrible if it did.

That was a dangerous train of thought considering he'd only just got rid of his morning boner. "Right, shower time!" Jackson jumped out of bed and picked up one of the towels that had been left out for them. "See you in a few."

AS THEY WENT DOWNSTAIRS, the sound of traditional Christmas carols spilled from the open kitchen door, and the smell of pancakes and coffee wafted through the hallway. Jackson's stomach rumbled in anticipation.

"Good morning. Happy Christmas!" Nick said as he walked through the doorway. "Do you need a hand with anything, Mum? It smells won— Oh!"

Reg was standing at the cooker, wearing pyjamas, dressing gown, slippers, and a Santa hat. He smiled. "Happy Christmas, you two. Did you sleep well?"

Nick seemed lost for words, so Jackson replied for both of them. "Yes, great thanks." His cheeks heated as he remembered Nick bouncing on the bed. He really hoped the creaking hadn't been too noticeable.

"Good, good."

"Where's Mum?" Nick asked.

"She's in the living room playing with Seth." Reg flipped over one of the pancakes. "He had Maria and Adrian up early so she's giving them a break. I'm in charge of breakfast this year."

"Oh, right. Well, it looks as if you've got everything under control. Can we just grab some coffee? Then we'll get out of your way and see if Mum needs an extra pair of hands."

"Actually, can you set the table first? That would be useful."

"Sure." Nick didn't sound too enthusiastic. "Are we having breakfast in the dining room or in here?"

"In here. It's warmer." He added more butter to the pan with a sizzle. "And there's coffee in the pot."

"Thanks." Nick poured out two mugs of coffee, added a spoonful of sugar to one and milk to both. "Here you go, babe." He handed the sweet one to Jackson.

"Thanks, hun." Jackson gave him a wicked grin.

"*Hun?*" Nick mouthed, wrinkling his nose in disgust.

Jackson bit back the urge to laugh at his expression. Hun was Nick's least favourite term of endearment. He cringed every time he heard anyone use it.

Nick opened a drawer, frowned and closed it again before trying the one next to it. "Where's the cutlery kept?"

"Hmm?" Reg turned. "Oh, yes. We keep them in that drawer now." He pointed to one on the other side of the kitchen. "Your mother rearranged everything years ago. I'd forgotten we ever kept them there."

"Well you did." Nick's voice was tight as he moved to the other drawer and started getting out knives and forks. He dumped them on the table with a clatter. "How about the plates, are they still in the same place?"

"I think so," Reg replied mildly. "Yes, that's right. The cupboard under the bread bin."

Jackson started laying out the cutlery, trying to ignore the tension that was mounting in the room.

Nick put a pile of plates on the table, and then he opened a few more cupboards and drawers, clearly searching for things, but he didn't ask Reg for any more help. Eventually he managed to gather placemats, glasses, and napkins. Jackson helped him lay everything out in silence.

"I think that's everything," Nick said.

"Yes, looks good. Thanks, boys. Tell your mother that everything will be ready in about ten minutes."

"Will do," Nick said, already on his way out of the kitchen.

Jackson sighed as he followed. He knew Nick had old grievances with his father, but he couldn't help wishing Nick would give him a chance. The man genuinely seemed to be trying hard to be nice, and Nick wasn't making it easy for him. Perhaps he wasn't being fair to Nick, but it was hard for Jackson to be objective given his own history.

In the living room, they found Sue sitting on the sofa with Seth on her lap, holding a little chunky cardboard book with slightly chewed corners.

"—and here's the cow. Look, Seth. What does a cow

say?" Seth looked at her expectantly. "Moooooo," she said. "Cows say moo. Moo moo!"

He smiled and his whole body wiggled with excitement as he echoed her. "Moo moo!"

"Yes!" She beamed. "That's right." Looking up, she greeted Jackson and Nick. "Happy Christmas! How are you two this morning?"

"Happy Christmas, Mum." Nick went over to sit beside her and let her lean across to kiss him on the cheek. He seemed to be softening towards his mother at least.

"Happy Christmas, Sue." Jackson took the seat beside Nick, who took his hand and casually threaded their fingers together. The warmth of his palm and the sight of their linked hands made Jackson's heart beat a little faster.

"Dad said breakfast will be ready in about ten minutes. Speaking of breakfast, since when did Dad cook?" Nick asked. "He could barely boil an egg when I was growing up."

"It started when he retired," she replied. "But he really got into it since he stopped drinking. It's become quite a hobby now, along with his art."

"His what?" Nick gaped at her.

"Art. He's been taking evening classes. Started out with watercolours but now he's branching out. Didn't you see the paintings in your room?"

"I saw them, but I had no clue they were Dad's. They're good!"

"Don't sound so surprised." Her lips quirked in amusement. "You've seen my attempts at drawing, so it stands to reason that you must have got your artistic talent from somewhere."

Seth tugged at the book impatiently. "Ma-ma-ma-ma!"

"Sorry, darling. I got distracted." She let him turn the page.

"Oof oof oof!" He flapped his chubby hands in excitement, looking up at her for confirmation.

"Yes! It's a dog. Woof woof. Clever boy."

NICK WAS UNUSUALLY quiet during breakfast. Jackson kept trying to catch his eye but Nick's gaze stayed on his food. He spent more time cutting his pancake and fruit into bits and pushing them around than he did eating, and left most of it on his plate.

"Are you all right, Nick?" Sue asked. "Don't you like the pancakes? You can make yourself some toast instead if you want."

"I'm just not very hungry."

"Too much wine last night?" Reg suggested with a grin. "At least you made it to breakfast. That's more than can be said for your brother."

"It's nothing to do with the wine." Nick glared at him. "Like I said, I'm just not hungry. And you're a fine one to judge Pete for drinking too much. I wonder where he learnt that behaviour?"

Reg's smile vanished. Sue cut in quickly. "Nick! That's enough."

"No, Sue, it's fine." Reg put a hand on her arm. "I deserved that." Silence hung heavy in the air as he met Nick's gaze unflinchingly. Even Seth was watching them, eyes intent and brow furrowed as though he was picking up on the emotions swirling around the room. "Yes. I used to drink too much, and I'm not proud of it, and I'm not judging anyone else. I'm sorry if it sounded that way."

A flush rose up Nick's face, turning even his ears pink as he cast his eyes down again. "Yeah." He shrugged. "It did a bit."

Reg waited, as though hoping for more from him, but nothing was forthcoming.

Jackson clenched his hands into fists. Warring emotions rose from his chest, tightening his throat and pounding at his temples. He wanted to be supportive of his friend, but he also wanted Nick to stop behaving like a petulant child and meet his father halfway. It stung that Nick had a chance at rebuilding this relationship when Jackson's dad was gone for good.

"Are we finished now?" Sue said.

Everyone answered in the affirmative, probably all as keen to break up the awkward atmosphere around the table and escape as Jackson was. He stayed long enough to do a little clearing away, before making his excuses and heading up to the bathroom on the top floor to brush his teeth.

When he was done, he didn't feel quite ready for more of Nick's family dynamics just yet, so he went into the bedroom and stood with his hands on the windowsill, staring out. It was a cold morning with a pale grey sky, thick frost coated the grass like icing sugar, and the bright disc of the sun was faintly visible through a thin veil of cloud.

Jackson's breath misted the glass as he sighed.

He wished he'd never agreed to come here. He longed for the relaxed atmosphere of his mum's house. With his family, any disagreements were superficial and were dealt with fast. This place was full of deep murky undercurrents, where old wounds and grievances constantly threatened to surface, like sharks looking for their next meal.

Anger still simmered in Jackson's veins, so when he heard the door open he didn't turn to greet Nick's friendly, "Hey."

"Hello." He tightened his grip on the windowsill.

"I was wondering where you'd disappeared to. What are you doing?"

"Nothing. I just needed a bit of peace for a minute."

"What's up?" Nick moved to stand beside him and nudged him gently with his shoulder.

Jackson gritted his teeth and took a slow breath while he tried to decide how honest to be. *Fuck it.* This was Nick. He was Jackson's best friend, and Jackson didn't want to keep this in. If he did, it would eat away at him all day and make him feel worse than he already did.

"I'm finding the whole thing with you and your dad really difficult." He kept staring out over the trees behind the house, unwilling to meet Nick's eyes. "The sniping and tension. It's... hard to watch."

"Yeah, I'm sorry. I know it's awkward. But you know how I feel about him, so what were you expecting?"

Jackson turned to face him. "I was expecting your dad to be a grade A arsehole, so I thought it would be easy to be on your side. Not that it's about taking sides.... But, Nick, I dunno. I just think you should give him a chance."

There was silence. Nick drew away from him, eyes tense and wary. "Give him a chance at what? It's not like he's asking me for forgiveness. I haven't even heard an apology from him yet—not for anything that happened in the past anyway."

"But he's trying to build bridges. I can see it in the way he is with you. Maybe he really has changed, Nick. I think you should talk to him, at least. Be honest about how he hurt you and let him have the opportunity to make amends."

It wasn't as if they'd fallen out over one specific event or at one particular time. Nick's relationship with his father had bled out slowly over many years. A thousand tiny wounds, each one superficial on its own, had been devastating in combination. Maybe Nick believed there was nothing left to save. But Jackson didn't think it was unfixable, not after meeting Reg.

"I don't want to fucking talk to him." His voice was icy. "And I certainly don't want to drag up all the ways he hurt me in the past. I don't trust him. Why would I want to make myself vulnerable again when I've spent years protecting myself from him? Why the fuck would you even suggest that? You're my friend. You're supposed to be on my side—and yes. It *is* about taking sides."

Jackson felt a stab of guilt. "Shit, Nick. I'm sorry. I am on your side okay? I just want what's best for you—and I thought that giving your dad a chance might not be such a bad idea. I thought maybe you could salvage a relationship with him. But maybe my judgement's clouded on this, because...." His voice cracked, and he paused to try to swallow down the sudden lump in his throat.

The anger on Nick's face melted away into understanding and compassion. "Because your dad isn't around at all anymore." Nick finished the sentence for him. "Jackson, I'm sorry. I wasn't thinking." He opened his arms and moved swiftly, pulling Jackson into a fierce hug. "I was too busy thinking about myself and my daddy issues to spare any thought for you, and how triggering this might be for you. I'm sorry, man. I'm sorry for being a shitty friend."

"'S okay," Jackson managed, his throat was tight and he squeezed his eyes shut to try to hold back the tears. "I didn't realise it would be hard either… until it was." He lost the battle against the emotions welling up inside him and a choked sob escaped.

Jackson had been six years old when the plane had crashed on a military training mission, killing his father and all the other occupants. When he tried to conjure up the hazy memories of his dad now, he saw a man who was like a giant, towering over him with a wide, kind smile. He remembered strong arms scooping him up, and sitting on his dad's shoulders, looking down on the world in delight, yelling, "I'm taller than you now, Daddy!"

His father had laughed, a deep warm chuckle. "Maybe one day you will be, kiddo."

Jackson had grown taller than his father sometime between his sixteenth and seventeenth birthdays, but his father hadn't been around to see it happen.

He burrowed into the comfort of Nick's arms, and Nick held him tight while his tears flowed.

SEVEN

The living room had barely changed in the years Nick had stayed away. Almost everything was the same from the patterned carpet, which hid a multitude of stains, to the pictures on the walls, to the now slightly faded sofas. With the Christmas tree in the bay window and the fire crackling in the grate, Nick could imagine he'd been transported back fifteen or twenty years. Even the fireguard that he remembered from his childhood was back, keeping Seth away from the flames, and the tinsel on the mantlepiece was probably the same piece they'd had for twenty years.

As he waited for the rest of his family to assemble to open their presents, Nick felt an unexpected wave of excitement, a nostalgic echo of all the times they'd waited impatiently as kids. Pete was the one who'd usually been bouncing on the sofa and yelling, "Hurry up!" to whichever parent was dragging their heels.

The current day version of Pete had just collapsed into an armchair, still looking rather rough around the edges despite the fact that he was dressed and showered. Adrian and Maria were sitting on the sofa with Seth, trying to keeping him entertained with a toy phone. Seth seemed more interested in chewing the phone than he did pressing the buttons.

"Right, can someone go and drag your father out of the kitchen, seeing as the rest of us are all here?" Nick's mother asked.

Pete didn't look as if he was willing to move, and Maria had Seth in her lap, so Nick said reluctantly, "Yeah, okay."

He found his father with his arm inside a turkey. "Dad?"

"What?" He glanced up, pink-cheeked and slightly harassed looking.

"Mum sent me to fetch you. Everyone's waiting to open presents."

"Bloody hell! Is it that time already? I need to finish stuffing this bird and get it in the oven first. I'll be as quick as I can."

"Okay." Poised to escape back to the living room, Nick remembered his earlier conversation with Jackson. Maybe it wouldn't kill him to make a little more effort. "Is there anything I can help with?"

"Oh, yes please. Could you stir the soup for me please? I think I left the heat a bit high and I'm worried the potatoes will stick."

"Sure." Nick went to the cooker and took the lid off a large saucepan, releasing a waft of fragrant steam. "Smells good. Is this for lunch?"

"Yes. It's nothing fancy. Just leek and potato."

"Nice." Nick stirred. It was catching a little on the bottom, but he'd got there in time. "Look at you, cooking soup and stuffing turkeys singlehanded. It's like real-life *MasterChef* in here."

His father gave a surprised chuckle. "Ha. I'm not sure about that. But hopefully it will all be edible, at least. If not, I'll probably be fired as head chef and your mother will take over again next year."

"Well, the soup is safe. I've turned it down now. Do you need a hand with anything else?"

He glanced up and gave him a quick, warm smile. "No thanks, Nick. But I appreciate the offer. Go and tell Mum I'll be there in a few minutes."

"Will do." Nick noticed it was starting to feel natural using *Mum* and *Dad* for them again, the old familiar names for them slipping out more easily.

ONCE THEY WERE ALL GATHERED, they began opening gifts.

Nick received predictable stuff from his family, typically unimaginative but useful things like gloves, a scarf, and a nice pen. And Jackson was given similar things. In some cases they got joint gifts, such as a bottle of gin from Pete. His parents had also given them a £200 John Lewis voucher as a joint gift. "I know it's terribly boring, but I had no idea what to get you," his mum said apologetically.

"No, thank you. That's really useful. We can buy something nice for the flat, can't we?" Nick said to Jackson, putting a casual hand on his thigh. "We were talking about getting a new sofa, so it could go towards that maybe."

"Yes, that's a great idea." Jackson smiled at Nick's parents. "Thanks."

Nick had bought boringly safe gifts for everyone in his family and had labelled them *from Nick and Jackson*, which had felt very odd to write when he'd wrapped them the day before Christmas Eve. Yet as his family opened them and thanked them both, it felt strangely natural to be addressed as a couple.

The gifts he received from Jackson were much more personal: the next book in a series he'd been reading, a DVD box set of the *Iron Man* movies, and finally a five-pack of boxer briefs that were the same as some that Jackson owned—only in different designs and colours.

"Oh, brilliant. Thanks. I love this brand."

"I noticed. That's why I've bought you your own set in the hopes that you'll stop borrowing mine all the time," Jackson said.

Nick grinned. "I can't promise, but it might help."

"That's one of the downsides of being in a same-sex relationship I'd never thought about," Maria said. "Thankfully I don't have to worry about Adrian borrowing my favourite knickers."

"How do you know he doesn't?" Nick asked. "Maybe he just washes them and puts them back before you notice they're gone."

"Oi!" Adrian protested. "I'll have you know I never borrow her knickers. They're too small for me, so I had to buy my own."

Everyone fell about laughing at that, even Seth, although he clearly had no idea what the joke was.

Nick had picked gifts for Jackson that he knew he needed or wanted. A new game, a stainless-steel water bottle for the gym, and some running socks because Nick had noticed his old ones had holes in.

"Perfect, thank you. I'd been meaning to get some for ages but I kept forgetting."

"You can finally bin the old ones now."

It didn't take long for everyone to finish opening all their presents. Seth had more gifts than anyone else, but he had his parents to help. Predictably, Seth was more interested in the wrapping paper and boxes than their contents.

"Right." Nick's dad stood. "That soup should be ready by now. I'll go and blend it. Can someone set the table for lunch?"

"I'll do that." Nick's mum got up too. "Please can you lot tidy up in here? Make sure you put the paper in the recycling."

AFTER LUNCH there was a lull in the day. The turkey was in the oven, and there was nothing else that needed doing immediately for dinner. Seth got taken upstairs for a nap, and Maria and Adrian disappeared along with him and never came back.

"I expect they're napping too," Nick's mum said with a yawn. "I don't blame them. He was up early, the little monkey." She yawned again. "Golly, I'm going to end up falling asleep on this sofa if I don't move. I fancy some fresh air and a stretch of the old legs. Does anyone want to join me for a walk?" She stood.

"Not me," Nick's dad said. "I need to baste the turkey again in half an hour, and I want to try and finish this damn crossword."

"Oh, go on then." Pete uncurled himself from an armchair. "It'll probably make me feel better. I can walk off the remainder of last night's toxins before we open the wine later."

"Nick, Jackson? How about you?" his mum asked.

"Yes, I wouldn't mind a walk." Nick took Jackson's hand, enjoying the sensation of Jackson's warm skin against his as he interlaced their fingers. "Do you fancy getting out for a bit?"

"I'd love to, but I want to call my family, and now is probably a good time. Do you mind if I stay here?" He said it in a teasing tone, but he squeezed Nick's hand gently and his eyes asked the same question in a more serious way.

Nick pressed his free hand against his heart. "Well, it'll be tough being without you all that time... but I'll find a way to cope." He leant across and kissed Jackson lightly on the lips, feeling a little thrill at the contact. "See you later, babe." He stood, releasing Jackson's hand. "Send my love to the family."

"Will do. Have a good walk, hun."

Pete made a puking sound. "You two aren't helping my hangover."

"You're just jealous," Nick said as they left the living room.

"Nope. I'm very happy being young, free, and single, thanks."

"You're not as young as you used to be, dickhead." He aimed a playful poke at Pete's ribs. He and his brother had spent so many years winding each other up that it was second nature to slip back into that pattern, like putting old comfortable shoes on.

Pete jabbed him back. "Thanks for the reminder, penis breath."

"Now, now, boys. That's enough," their mum said from behind them.

Nick stuck his tongue out at Pete, who responded in kind by grimacing and crossing his eyes.

"Honestly. You two. I'd forgotten what you used to be like."

Their mum's tone of exasperated amusement made them both laugh.

"I blame the parents." Pete winked at Nick and held his hand up for a high five.

Nick grinned and slapped his hand, suddenly realising that he'd missed Pete, even though he was a dickhead.

JACKSON WENT UPSTAIRS for some privacy while he video called his family. It was lovely to see their faces and talk to them, but it made him miss them even more than he already did. It felt so wrong not being there for Christmas this year. He could hear the kids playing in the background, excited shrieks and giggles.

"We miss you so much, honey," his mum said. "And Nick too. It's not the same without you here."

"Yeah. It's not," his sister Ruby chimed in. "But you're coming for New Year, right? So we'll see you both then?"

"Yes, that's the plan."

"What's it like there?" his mum asked. "I hope it's going okay. How's Nick getting on with his dad?" She knew Nick had a difficult relationship with his dad. Not that they talked about it much, but when Jackson had brought Nick home for Christmas that first year when he couldn't face going home it had been obvious. Jackson's mum had welcomed him with open arms, and over the years Nick had become almost as much a part of the family as Jackson was.

"Things are still pretty tense between them," Jackson replied.

"Oh. I'm sorry to hear that."

Ruby popped into the frame again, asking, "What's his dad like? Is he awful?"

"Not really. He's definitely nothing like as bad as I imagined, but I think he's changed a lot since they fell out. Seems to me like he's trying to heal the rift, but Nick's not very receptive." He gave a huff of frustration. "I wish he'd lower his guard a bit."

"It's hard when someone's been hurt, though," his mum said gently. "It's only natural that Nick would be defensive. He's just trying to protect himself."

"Yeah. I know. But I reckon he'll regret it one day if he doesn't accept the olive branch his old man's waving at him."

"Give them time, love. Maybe that's what Nick needs."

"Yeah." It was all Jackson could do. It wasn't like he could force Nick to kiss and make up with his dad.

They talked for a while longer and when it was time to go, Jackson blew them all kisses and wished them all a merry Christmas again before ending the call.

The house was very quiet as he made his way downstairs. The living room was empty, so he guessed the walkers were still out. Christmas choral music was coming from the kitchen again, so he went in there and found Reg peeling potatoes.

"Hello. I thought you were finishing your crossword," Jackson said.

"I've done it!" Reg said triumphantly. "The whole damn thing. It was the Christmas special so it was twice the size of normal."

"Well done."

"Yes. It feels like quite an achievement." He beamed.

Jackson wanted an excuse to chat to him a little more, and he had a feeling Reg would refuse help if it was offered, so he decided not to give him the choice. He'd noticed a drawer full of utensils when he'd helped clear away after lunch, so he got out another vegetable peeler and joined Reg at the island in the middle of the kitchen.

"Oh, thanks," Reg said as Jackson picked up a potato. He looked a little surprised, but he didn't object.

They worked in silence for a few minutes, until Reg asked, "So... you and Nick. Have you been together long?"

"Uh. Not that long really?" Jackson felt his cheeks heat. "Less than a year."

"But you live together. Is that right?"

"We lived together anyway." Inwardly, he was cursing Nick for putting him in this position. He hated lying and had always been fairly terrible at it. "We've been friends for a long time." At least that much was true.

"That's good. Sue and I were friends first too. I think it makes a solid basis for a relationship."

"I'm sure it—I mean, yes. It absolutely does."

"It's good to see Nick looking happy." Reg picked up

another potato from the pile. "Well, if truth be told, it's good to see him at all. I wasn't sure he'd come."

"He did need a bit of persuading."

"So I heard." Reg's tone was serious. When Jackson chanced a sideways glance at him, his mouth was drawn down at the corners. "I'm glad he's here, but I wish he'd let go of the past and relax a little."

Jackson took a deep breath, hoping he wasn't about to make an already tricky situation worse. "Reg, with respect, why don't you try talking to him about it?" He bit back the urge to tell him he should apologise. "I know Nick, and he might be very good at holding a grudge, but he's also good at giving people chances. He's guarded, though, and he doesn't trust people easily. So if you really want to fix things with him, you'll need to make the first move."

He stopped, heart beating fast.

Reg was silent for a long moment. "Thank you for your honesty," he finally said. "And you're right. I do need to talk to him. I know I was hard on him when he was young. I tried to push him into being someone he wasn't, and all I succeeded in doing was driving him away." He gave a dry huff of laughter that had no joy in it. "The irony is that he's achieved so much, without any support from me. I'm so proud of him for the way he's carved out his own path and done so well for himself."

"You should tell him that," Jackson said. "I think he'd like to hear it."

"Yes. You're right. I'll talk to him when he gets back." He put his peeler down and clapped Jackson on the shoulder. "Thanks, Jackson. You're a good man." He gave Jackson's shoulder a quick squeeze as he added gruffly, "I'm glad Nick's found someone like you."

Complicated emotions rushed through Jackson: pride, guilt, and a wistful longing that almost choked him. "I'm lucky to have him," he managed. In that moment he realised that he wished with all his heart that this pretence was the truth.

I'm in love with Nick. The realisation struck a blow to Jackson's chest, stealing his breath. It was as though a lens had fallen into place and all his feelings suddenly slid into painfully clear focus. This wasn't a crush. This was the real deal, only he hadn't wanted to see it. *Holy fucking shit. I'm in love with Nick and I had no idea.*

He also had no idea what to do with the information now his unconscious mind had finally let it surface. So he picked up another potato and carried on peeling, wondering when exactly he had fallen in love with his best friend, and how he'd managed to hide it from himself for so long.

JACKSON AND REG had finished peeling and chopping all the potatoes, then worked their way through the carrots, and were busy tackling a pile of Brussels sprouts when the sound of the back door alerted them to the walkers arriving home.

"The wanderers return," Reg said lightly. "Did you have a nice walk?"

"Yes, it was lovely," Sue replied. "Gosh! Haven't you two been busy. Well done."

"We went to the Pirate Tree," Pete said. With his

cheeks pink from the cold, he looked a lot brighter than he had before they'd left. "I can't believe how good it's looking. I thought it would have fallen apart by now."

"I've been taking care of it," Reg said. "I've fixed it up a few times over the years and treated the wood when it needed it."

"Why?" Nick asked, his face intent. A strand of bright hair had fallen over his forehead. "Why would you bother?"

Reg shrugged. "We put a lot of work into making it. It seemed a shame to let it rot. Seth might want to play in it when he's bigger, and maybe there'll be other grandchildren eventually."

"Not from me." Pete wrinkled his nose. "I don't think I have a paternal bone in my body. But I'm sure Maria and Adrian want more sprogs. How about you two?" He glanced from Nick to Jackson and back again as he asked casually, "Do you want kids?"

Jackson's heart skipped a beat.

"We haven't talked about it yet," Nick said smoothly. "But who knows? Maybe one day." He smiled, a sweet intimate smile that made Jackson's chest ache with all the things he'd been secretly longing for and never known about. His heart felt as if it had been torn wide open and all those hidden desires were flooding out like a river, threatening to sweep him away.

Somehow he managed to force himself to smile back.

"Maybe," he said.

EIGHT

Nick was in the living room with Jackson, Seth, and Maria. The Queen was on TV making her annual Christmas speech. "She's amazing, isn't she?" Nick marvelled at Her Majesty. "I swear she doesn't seem to have got any older since I was a kid. How is that possible?"

"Portrait in the attic?" Jackson suggested.

"Good genes?" Maria said. "The Queen Mother was incredible too."

"Nick?" His dad's voice from the doorway tore Nick's attention away from pondering on the Queen's miraculous longevity. "Can I have a word?" Something about his tone made Nick's anxiety spike. "In private," he added.

Nick's stomach lurched. "Yeah, okay." He kept his voice deliberately casual as he stood and stretched, before following his dad out of the room.

"We'll talk in my study."

Those words had Nick's muscles tightening defensively. As he crossed the threshold into the forbidding gloom of the study, the dark wood-panelled walls seemed to close in around him, resonating with layer upon layer of unhappy memories of all the times his school reports had been unsatisfactory—so probably at the end of every term.

This isn't good enough, Nick.

You need to buckle down.

Don't you want to go to a good university?

Stop wasting your potential!

He shoved his hands in his pockets and stood, waiting for his dad to take a seat behind his desk. But instead, he surprised Nick by leaning on the edge of the desk so they were face-to-face. A muscle ticked in his jaw and he looked down for a moment. He seemed to be even more nervous than Nick.

"Nick," he began. "I'm glad you're here for Christmas this year." He looked up and met Nick's eyes. "It's been too long, and I hope this will be the first of many more. I know you've been angry with me for a long time, and I don't blame you. My drinking made me a difficult person to live with. I was stressed and unhappy and I took that out on the people I loved." Nick held his gaze and waited, wondering what else would be forthcoming. "And I'm sorry that I wasn't more supportive when you came out. I was shocked, honestly." He shrugged. "I never saw it coming, and I didn't know how to react. I didn't disapprove, I was just... blindsided I suppose, so I didn't know the right things to say."

"Yeah. You really didn't," Nick said bitterly.

Are you sure?

Maybe you're just confused.

How can you really know at your age?

Have you ever tried it with a girl?

None of those things were on the list of supportive things to say to a gay son when he came out of the closet.

"I let you down, and I'm sorry. I love you, Nick, and I'm so proud of you and what you've done with your life. It's wonderful to see the success you've made of your business, and now in your personal life... settling down with a lovely man like Jackson."

His dad's expression was painfully genuine, and somehow that only made Nick's anger burn more brightly. He clung to his fury, reluctant to let it go, feeding it with all the dark echoes of the past that had been stirred up. "I don't care what you think!" he flung the words out like sharp things that could wound. "I don't need your approval now. I don't *need* you to be proud of me. Your opinion means nothing to me because I stopped caring what you thought of me a long time ago."

He clenched his fists into furious balls, shouting now and not caring who might overhear. "It's too fucking late! I needed it then, not now. When I was growing up I was never clever enough, never hard-working enough, never sporty enough. Pete was the golden boy and I was the one who never lived up to your expectations, who never achieved his full potential, just because I wanted to study art instead of maths, and I didn't want to be a bloody accountant or financial advisor or whatever else you wanted me to be. I was never allowed to follow my *own* dreams. You made me feel like shit, like I was *never* good enough. I needed you to love me for who I was, to accept me as I was, and you didn't, and you can't go back and fix that."

He stared at his dad's shocked face, his heart racketing

around behind his ribs like a rat trapped in a cage. Nick was shocked too. He hadn't realised the full extent of his anger until he'd unleashed it. Now he'd got it out of his system, all the fight had left him in a rush and he felt weak and shaky.

"Nick," his dad's voice was hoarse. "I didn't know... I never meant...." He drew a harsh breath. "I didn't realise I made you feel like that. I just wanted what was b—what *I* thought was best for you." He gave a sad smile. "Turns out you knew what was best all along."

Nick snorted, surprised by the admission. "Yeah. I guess I did."

"And you're right. I can't go back and fix it. All I can do is tell you that I'm truly sorry, and that I love you, and that I'd like us to start over if you're able to forgive me."

The words hung there. Branches of possibility spread in front of Nick, and his chest felt closed and tight as he considered them. He was so wary of making himself vulnerable again. But he wasn't a child any longer. He was a grown man who had dealt with a lot of his own shit over the last two years. And if his dad's open-hearted apology was anything to go by, it seemed Nick wasn't the only one to have done some soul-searching.

Nick drew in a breath. The cage around his heart creaked open, not fully, but enough for him to take the risk. "I'll give it a go." It was the best he could offer.

His dad's face softened into a hopeful smile. "That's all I ask."

They stared at each other and Nick felt the walls of resentment begin to crumble. It would take time for them to fall away completely, but for the first time in years Nick was able to imagine a time when they might. The moment drew out, and Nick began to feel uncomfortable. Should he offer his dad a hug? He didn't think he was ready for that, so he let his gaze slide away and looked around the study, searching for distraction.

It was very different from the room he remembered. The decor was the same, but the walls were covered with pictures. At first Nick didn't make the connection until he looked more closely and recognised his mum in a charcoal drawing, a sleeping Seth in a pencil sketch, and his parents' house and garden brought to life in watercolours.

"These are yours?" he said incredulously.

"Yes."

Nick studied an acrylic painting of a vase of daffodils. "They're bloody good," he said begrudgingly. "I mean, it's not quite Van Gogh...."

His dad laughed. "Not even close."

"But seriously. They're great. How did you keep this talent a secret all this time?"

"I didn't know I had a talent for it. Not really. I always loved drawing as a child, but I was never encouraged to pursue it. Your grandfather didn't think it was a suitable hobby." A twisted smile. "I expect that sounds familiar. They say that patterns repeat through generations. I wish I'd been enlightened enough to break the mould."

Nick was suddenly shot through with compassion for that younger version of his dad, another boy who wasn't given permission to follow his dreams.

At least Nick had rebelled early enough that it hadn't held him back.

"Better late than never?" Nick offered.

This time his dad's smile was easy and light. He chuckled. "Indeed."

There was an easel near the window, and Nick moved to look at the unfinished acrylic painting that stood on it. It depicted an ancient oak tree. The huge trunk twisted and spiralled upwards, opening out branches to the sky. There was a hole in the trunk, in a shape and location that Nick recognised immediately. "You're painting the Pirate Tree!"

"Yes."

"I love it. You've got the texture of the trunk just right. It makes me almost feel it in my fingertips."

"Thanks." His ears had turned pink from the praise. "I'm very happy with this one so far." Then he looked at his watch. "Oh, damn it. Is that the time? I must go and baste the turkey again and get the potatoes boiling. Sorry."

"No problem. I don't want to hold up the chef." Nick grinned.

"Thanks, Nick. I'm glad we talked."

"Me too."

Nick stayed behind after his dad had gone, taking his time to look at all the pictures that covered the walls of the study. It was going to take him a while to get used to this new version of his dad, but he reckoned they were going to get along okay.

He returned to the painting of the Pirate Tree last and tried to imagine how it would look when it was finished. He'd have to ask his dad to send him a photo of it. It was such a brilliant place. For a long time it had been Nick's favourite place in the world. He wished Jackson had had a chance to see it in daylight yesterday.

The very moment that thought passed through his

mind, a shaft of late afternoon sunlight lit the canvas as the sun emerged from beneath the blanket of cloud that had covered the sky all day. Suddenly the picture seemed more alive, the colours brighter and more vibrant, beckoning to him like a sign from the universe.

If they were quick, they'd get there before it was dark.

He went to find Jackson. "I fancy another walk. Do you want to come?"

"Sure. Especially as I missed out earlier."

"Hurry then, before it gets dark. We should probably both take our phones today, just in case." Nick didn't ask if anyone else wanted to join them, and luckily nobody suggested it.

They wrapped up warm and let themselves out of the back door.

Nick set a brisk pace through the woods as the sun dropped lower in the sky, the yellow light slanting through the bare branches.

"How did the conversation go with your dad?" Jackson asked as he followed close behind Nick along the narrow path.

"It was good," Nick said. "Surprisingly good in the end."

"Yeah? That's awesome. So did you make up with him?"

"Yes. I suppose I did. He apologised a bit, and I yelled at him. Then he apologised again... for the things that actually mattered." He rounded on Jackson. "Did you talk to him while I was out earlier? About me, I mean."

Jackson's expression told Nick everything he needed

even before he answered. "Yes. I hope you're not mad with me? I know I shouldn't have interfered, but—"

"Hey." Nick put a hand on his shoulder. "It's okay. I know you were trying to help, and look. It worked." He smiled. "You were right about me giving him a chance. I'm glad I did. I think things are going to be all right between the two of us going forward, and that means I get my family back."

He threw his arms around Jackson and hugged him, holding on until Jackson brought his arms up and hugged Nick back.

"Thank you," Nick said softly. His face was pressed into the skin of Jackson's neck just above his scarf. He inhaled the sweet musky scent, and his heart swelled with affection and gratitude. "Thank you so much for every-thing. For being here. For helping me sort things out with my dad. You're the best."

"It's nothing," Jackson said gruffly. He squeezed Nick a little tighter. "I know you'd do the same for me."

"In a heartbeat." Nick released him, reluctant to leave the comforting warmth of his arms. But the light was starting to fade, and they had a tree to find. "I love you, man." He'd said the same thing to Jackson often enough over the course of their friendship that it shouldn't have felt strange. But somehow today the words took on new reso-nance, hanging between them in the twilight as Jackson hesitated for a moment before replying.

"I love you too."

As they continued through the woods, Nick said, "How would you feel about staying here an extra night? I was thinking about asking Mum and Dad if that's okay. There's nothing you have to get back for tomorrow, is there? I know Maria and Adrian are here until the twenty-ninth, and it would be nice to have more time with them... and Pete too, I think he's staying tomorrow night." It would also be good to have more time to get to know his dad again, and help to build their new tenuous connection.

"Yes, that's fine."

"Are you sure?" The path was wider here, and he glanced sideways so he could see Jackson beside him.

"Yeah. There's nothing I need to get back for—apart from the gym. And I can live without that for another day."

"You could go running with Adrian and Pete, while I keep your spot on the sofa warm."

Jackson laughed. "You're so kind."

Nick had never been a runner. He still preferred dancing over any other exercise, but he kept himself fit by swimming a couple of times a week and walking or cycling rather than driving wherever possible.

"Here we are." Nick stopped at the base of the Pirate Tree. "Isn't it beautiful?"

"Yes." Jackson stared up into the branches. "It's pretty awesome."

Nick took his gloves off and put his hands on the gnarled trunk. "How old do you think it is?"

"I dunno. Must be close to a hundred years old, given the size of it. Maybe more?"

It was strange to think that there was so much more of it beneath the surface, the roots growing and spreading through a secret subterranean world, invisible anchors that had held the tree strong and steady through countless storms. The thought sent a strange tingle up Nick's spine, as though he was absorbing some ancient energy from the earth.

"Are you okay?"

"Yeah. Yeah I'm good." Nick shook off the strange feeling. "Let's climb. Do you want to go first this time?"

"No, I'm happy following."

"You just want the excuse to look at my arse," Nick teased, grinning.

"Well, it is pretty easy on the eye." Jackson's tone was light, but he avoided Nick's gaze. "Plus I'll be able to check where the footholds are." He got his phone out and turned the torch on ready.

Nick climbed up easily, the pattern of movement easy and familiar. Muscle memory was an amazing thing, laid down years ago in nerve pathways that branched in his brain much like the roots of the tree he was climbing.

When he reached the platform, he looked down to see Jackson standing inside the tree, cramped in the tight space as he shone his torch towards his feet.

"Can you see what you're aiming for?" Nick asked.

"Yeah. I think I've got it this time." Jackson put his torch away to climb. "Ugh. I'm too big for this."

"You managed it last time. You're fine."

"It would be a hell of a lot easier if I was skinny. My shoulders don't give me much room to manoeuvre. Oof. Nearly there."

He finally hauled himself out into the open and sat beside Nick, breathless and grinning. "Made it."

"Well done." Nick patted him on the back.

"And it was totally worth it." Jackson looked around. "It's cool to see it in daylight. What a place!"

"It's perfect, isn't it?"

The tree cradled them, holding them between the earth and the sky. At this time of year, the branches were bare enough for them to see the orange and pink of the sunset through the surrounding trees.

"It's so peaceful." Jackson sat motionless with a faraway look on his face.

Nick tuned in to the sounds of nature around them: the whispering of a few determined leaves still clinging to the branches, the sudden rustle of a squirrel in a neighbouring tree, the birdsong that would soon fade with the light. The tingling sensation of before returned, a sense of connection to the world around him borne on a swooping rush of happiness. He let his gaze settle on Jackson, and the feeling built, swelling in his chest and making his heart beat faster.

"Are you okay?" Jackson looked at him curiously. "You look... I dunno. As if you're about to cry, or maybe burst into song or something."

"Yeah. I'm fine. Just... glad to be here." The feeling was too elusive, too intangible, and too precious to even attempt to describe properly. He wanted to guard it and keep it safe, not dilute it into inadequate words.

Self-conscious, he broke eye contact to gaze into the branches above him. "Oh look!" He chuckled, pointing at the spherical tangle of leaves that hung a few metres above their heads. "Mistletoe. It's such a shame we're not really a couple, otherwise this would be the most perfect thing in the world, wouldn't it?" He grinned at Jackson. "Alone in this beautiful place, birds singing, the sun setting, a ball of mistletoe right there. It's as if the universe was planning this especially for us." Despite his attempt at humour,

Nick's heart thumped extra hard and there was a strange swoopy feeling in his stomach.

Jackson glanced up and then gave Nick an uneasy smile. "Yeah." His huff of laughter didn't quite ring true.

"It honestly feels as if we're supposed to kiss right now. Like it's somehow meant to happen." Nick wasn't joking anymore. They stared at each other, trapped by a strange intensity that seemed to buzz in the air around them, some ancient and inevitable force as old as nature itself.

"Go ahead and kiss me then." There was a hint of challenge in Jackson's eyes, as though he was daring Nick to do something dangerous.

Nick didn't hesitate. If he thought too hard, he would come up with a thousand reasons not to do it. Instead, he let instinct guide him as he slid closer, curled one hand around the back of Jackson's neck, and drew him in. As their mouths touched, the electrical sensation grew and spread. He softened his lips, allowing them to part against Jackson's for a moment, and to his amazement Jackson started to kiss him back in earnest. Slowly and gently, but with such utter determination that it made Nick's body light up from his toes to his scalp with a sweet rush of desire.

This is a terrible idea.

But it was too late for that now. Nick's rational mind would have had more luck stopping a juggernaut skidding out of control. He didn't want to pause even for a moment to question what they were doing in case this midwinter magic evaporated and the moment was lost. Driven by a heady cocktail of hormones and emotion he deepened the kiss, bringing his other hand to Jackson's cheek as Jackson wrapped his arms around Nick and tugged him closer.

The kiss had an edge of desperation to it as though neither of them wanted to let it end. Nick thought he would carry on kissing Jackson forever if he could. Caught in this perfect moment, he wasn't ready to deal with the inevitable fallout that would come when they stopped.

Jackson's stubble rubbed against Nick's and he gave a low, throaty moan that Nick echoed. He moved closer still, climbing awkwardly across so he could sit in Jackson's lap. With one hand tangled in Nick's hair, Jackson put his other hand on Nick's arse and hauled him closer till there was no space between them.

Jackson broke away to pant in Nick's ear. "Fuck, Nick. What the hell are we doing?"

"Snogging." Nick drew Jackson's mouth back to his and kissed him briefly again before pausing to mutter, "I'm sure you're familiar with the concept."

This time it was Jackson who reclaimed Nick's mouth for more kissing, so Nick was satisfied that whatever the hell they *were* doing, Jackson was on board with it too.

Thank fuck. His dick was hard enough to crack nuts on, and he hadn't had any sexual contact with another person for so long that he'd almost forgotten what it felt like. Unless Jackson actually told him in no uncertain terms that he wanted to stop, it would take an earthquake, or maybe a meteorite, to shift Nick off course now.

Reaching between them, he found a reassuring bulge in Jackson's jeans. Relieved he wasn't the only one who was horny, he managed to work Jackson's fly open with one hand. "Is this okay?" he muttered between kisses.

"Yeah," Jackson replied hoarsely, and then as Nick's fingers curled around his dick he exclaimed, "Fuck! Your hand's cold."

"Sorry." Nick laughed. "Hang on. Let's try this instead."

He gave Jackson one last quick kiss on the lips before sliding carefully off his lap, pausing to check there was a solid plank to crouch on. This would have been a very inopportune time to fall down the hole in the trunk. He pushed Jackson's knees apart and freed his cock. "Sorry," he said as Jackson yelped. "Cold hands, I know.... This'll feel better." He replaced his chilly fingers with his mouth, giving Jackson an experimental suck. For all his fussing about cold hands, the temperature didn't seem to have cooled Jackson's ardour. He was thick and hard, and felt so damn good in Nick's mouth.

"Fuck." Jackson slid his fingers into Nick's hair, stroking his scalp and then gripping as Nick sucked him deep. "Oh my God... Nick."

It was so strange hearing his best friend's voice saying his name with that desperate needy edge to it. It probably shouldn't have turned Nick on so much, but it did. He bobbed his head up and down, feeling Jackson start to meet his movements, thrusting up into Nick's throat. Desperate for some relief himself now, Nick rubbed his erection through his jeans, wondering how long it would take him to come in his pants if he carried on, and how uncomfortable it would be to walk back like that if he did.

"Fuck. That's so good. I'm not going to last much longer."

That was fine with Nick, because then maybe Jackson

would reciprocate and save his underwear from a sticky fate.

Nick gave a stifled moan of encouragement and redoubled his efforts until he was rewarded by Jackson gasping his name again. His fingers tightened in Nick's hair and his cock pulsed, filling Nick's mouth with come and almost choking him. He managed to wait till Jackson had finished before he pulled off and swallowed.

"God, Nick... that was... what the fuck just happened?" Jackson sounded dazed.

Desperate for his turn, Nick was already unbuttoning his jeans. "You just shot your load in the back of my throat, and I nearly shot mine in my pants." He wrapped his hand around himself, finding his cock sticky with precome. "Any chance you want to help me out here?"

"Yeah, sure."

"Hand or mouth?"

"Mouth, but I'm not sure my legs are working. Gimme a minute."

Nick didn't feel as if he had a minute to spare. He pulled himself up to stand astride Jackson's legs, hanging on tight to a couple of branches. He bent his knees slightly so his cock was level with Jackson's mouth. "How's this?"

"Yeah. That works."

"Awesome. Open up then." He bumped the tip of his cock against Jackson's mouth. "Ohhh, fuck." As wet warmth enveloped him he tightened his grip on the tree, praying the branches were as strong as they looked. "So good." Tragically this was going to be over way too soon, but it had been two years since anyone had sucked him off and the sensation was just too intense. He pushed instinctively into it, rocking his hips and trying to get deeper. "Gonna come," he muttered.

A couple more thrusts and he was there, crying out sharply as the overwhelming rush of orgasm tore through him. His legs nearly gave out, but Jackson's hands were there on his hips to hold him steady until the wave of climax had passed.

"Christ on a bike," Nick said weakly. He uncurled his hands from the death grip he had on the branches and let himself slide down until he was sitting in Jackson's lap. He rested his head on Jackson's shoulder and felt strong arms come up around him. "Fucking hell."

"You okay?" Jackson asked.

"Yeah." Nick had no idea whether he was okay, honestly. He'd just blown his best mate in a tree. It was going to take him a little while to integrate that experience and make sense of it. *Shit.* What would it mean for their friendship? That thought sent a jolt of anxiety through his stomach. "You?"

"I think so. I'm just trying to work out how the hell that happened. Am I awake? Because if not, then I'm having a very weird dream."

Nick gave a weak chuckle. "Well if it's a dream, I'm having it too."

Jackson laughed and the warm familiar sound was reassuring. Things might be a bit weird between them after this, but they'd work it out somehow.

They had to.

NINE

Jackson tightened his arms around Nick, trying to ignore his growing sense of unease at what they'd just done. All those years of friendship and then... *that*. What kind of insanity had gripped them both?

Time was ticking away, and they needed to get back for dinner soon. Jackson was unwilling to break the spell that still surrounded them. Wrapped in each other's arms like this, it was as though they were lovers in a storybook, bound together by something unbreakable with a happy-ever-after guaranteed. But that wasn't their reality.

He wished he knew what was going on in Nick's head. Was Jackson the only one who'd just been shaken to his foundations? Was he the only one who felt as if things could never be the same again—who didn't *want* things to ever be the same again?

"So... um. That was...." Words were too difficult.

"Fun?" Nick supplied.

Fun was one way of describing it. Mind-blowing would have been more accurate, and not just because it had felt so good. Jackson's brain was total mush in the aftermath, and his thoughts were anxious and scattered. "Oh yeah, for sure. But kinda crazy, huh?" Surely Nick had to be a little freaked out too?

"Mmm." Nick's sound of agreement was muffled by Jackson's shoulder.

Jackson wanted more of a response than that, but he was too afraid to ask anything too direct in case he didn't like the answer. "I'm pretty sure we just breached some best friends' contract or something."

Nick laughed. Raising his head to meet Jackson's gaze, his expression was bright and seemingly unconcerned. "Probably. But does it matter? We're still good, right?"

"Of course."

Face softening, Nick cupped Jackson's cheek and surprised him with a brief kiss on the lips. "We wouldn't be the first friends to fool around together. We're consenting adults, we're both single. It's not like it's hurting anyone."

Not yet. Jackson's heart warned him, jumping in his chest. "Of course not," he said.

"We've both been celibate for too long, and you've got to admit that was pretty great. Maybe we should just let ourselves enjoy it. It is Christmas after all." Nick smiled.

Jackson stared at him. Was he suggesting this could be more than a one off? "Do you mean... you might want to do that again?"

"Well, not that *exactly*. I don't want to push my luck and fall out of a tree in some embarrassing sexual misadventure." Nick's amused expression faded into hopeful uncertainty. "But something else maybe? We're sharing a bed for the next few nights... so we could see what happens with all that close proximity." He shrugged. "I'm up for it if you are. Think about it." With that, he got off Jackson's lap and started rearranging his clothes. "Come on. Time to head back."

JACKSON'S MIND was reeling as they walked through the darkening wood.

What exactly did Nick have in mind? The invitation to do more had been pretty clear, but did he only mean while they were sharing a bed here? And if Jackson let himself give in to temptation and agreed to it, what would happen when they got home?

They let themselves in through the back door and found Reg in the kitchen with his apron on and his sleeves rolled up. Every ring on the gas hob had a pan on it, the windows were steamed up, and the scent of roast turkey filled the room.

"Hello, boys," he greeted them. "Good timing. Dinner will be in about twenty minutes. The others opened some bubbly while you were out. It's in the living room along with the glasses."

"Lovely, thanks. Do you need some help?" Nick asked.

"No, it's all under control, thank you."

As they passed through the kitchen, Nick stopped and caught Jackson's sleeve. "Hey, not so fast." He pointed up with a mischievous grin.

Jackson glanced up at the mistletoe. "Again?" He raised his brows.

"It's traditional." The kiss was sweet and chaste, totally

unlike the frenzied kisses they'd recently shared in the tree, but it still made Jackson's heart beat faster.

"DINNER WAS FANTASTIC, Dad, thank you for cooking." Maria pushed her knife and fork together. "But I'm going to have to admit defeat, or I definitely won't have room for pudding."

"I'll have that potato." Adrian deftly swiped it from her plate. "They were delicious."

"Yes, Reg. You did a wonderful job," Sue said.

Preoccupied with thoughts of what he and Nick had done earlier and what they might do later, Jackson had barely tasted his turkey. He'd managed to get through the meal by pretending to listen to the conversation, while his thoughts ran around in endless circles never reaching any conclusions.

He knew that he absolutely shouldn't do anything else sexual with Nick, because it was a stupid idea. Their friendship was way too important to jeopardise. Perhaps Nick could cope with injecting a bit of casual sex into their relationship, but Jackson knew there was no way he could handle anything casual. Now he was finally being honest with himself, he could see that his feelings for Nick were too complicated already, and switching to some kind of fuck buddy relationship could only make things worse. In his heart, Jackson had to admit that he wanted far more than Nick appeared to be offering. But he was afraid to be honest with Nick about that, because he didn't think there was any chance that Nick felt the same. If Nick had those sorts of feelings for him, surely he wouldn't be suggesting they fool around, because it put the stakes way too high.

His attention was caught by Nick's voice. "Mum, Dad... is it okay if Jackson and I stay an extra night?"

"Of course, darling!" Sue answered immediately, her face lighting up. "That's fine, isn't it, Reg?"

"Absolutely. It will be nice to have you here for longer now we've finally got you back." Reg smiled at Nick, his expression warm and open.

Nick smiled back, cheeks flushing slightly. "Well, it seemed a shame for us to rush off tomorrow now we're here."

Jackson looked down at his plate and clenched one fist under the table where nobody could see. More time here meant more forced proximity, and more temptation to take whatever crumbs Nick was offering.

I am so screwed.

AFTER DINNER HAD BEEN CLEARED AWAY, they relaxed in front of the TV with cups of tea and watched *Monsters, Inc.* Once that was over Maria and Adrian put an overtired Seth to bed, and when they returned, Maria said, "Anyone fancy a game of Triv?"

"Yeah, okay," Nick said. "Are you in, babe?" He patted Jackson's knee.

"For sure." Trivial Pursuit was one of the games Jackson's family often played at Christmas too.

"Ugh. I guess." Pete yawned.

They all ended up playing, and decided to play in three

teams. Pete went with his parents, Maria with Adrian, and Jackson with Nick.

As the game progressed, Nick and Jackson made quick work of filling their playing piece with coloured wedges.

"I think you two have an unfair advantage," Pete said, as they claimed their fifth piece of pie. "Between you, you don't seem to have a weak spot. Nobody on our team is any good at the entertainment questions."

"Yeah, and we're both useless at the geography ones," Maria said. "You two are bound to win."

It was true, their areas of general knowledge complemented each other well. Nick was better with literature and entertainment, whereas Jackson was good on science, sport, and geography. They were both pretty decent at the history questions.

"Yeah. We are a good fit." Nick smiled at Jackson, and the warmth in his eyes lit an answering glow in Jackson's chest. "We're obviously made for each other."

Jackson deflated as he remembered Nick was putting on an act for his family.

But he wasn't acting in the treehouse earlier.

Although that thought was reassuring on some levels, it didn't fill the aching gap in Jackson's heart.

They did win the game, as predicted. But in a second round, Maria and Adrian managed to claw their way to victory.

"Right. I'm afraid that's it for me," Maria said. "I need to get off to bed, because no doubt Seth will wake us up at the crack of dawn again."

"Yes, me too." Adrian yawned.

Sue and Reg went up to bed too, leaving Jackson, Nick,

and Pete in front of the TV again. Nick snuggled up to Jackson, fitting himself under his arm and tucking his feet up. It felt so easy and natural, as if they sat like this every night.

Despite their relaxed position, Jackson was feeling increasingly jittery about the prospect of going to bed. What would happen when they did? What did he want to happen?

He let himself imagine various possibilities, sending a thrill of excitement through his body. If Nick initiated anything, Jackson knew he wouldn't be able to find the strength to resist—even though he knew it was probably a terrible idea. The realisation escaped in a shaky sigh.

"You okay, babe?" Nick said softly.

"Yeah."

"Tired?" Nick put a hand on Jackson's thigh, stroking him in a way that was more arousing than soothing.

"A bit." Jackson wasn't remotely tired if truth be told. As Nick's hand crept a little higher every cell in his body was on red alert, primed and tingling. Nick grabbed his dick, squeezing it through his jeans, and Jackson bit back a yelp of surprise, turning it into a cough at the last minute.

"Wanna head up to bed?" Nick gave him a suggestive grin.

"Yes." He shoved Nick's hand away, glancing nervously at Pete who was still fixated on the TV, oblivious to the sexual tension that was building fast on the other side of the room.

Nick got up and offered Jackson a hand, helping to pull him up as he said cheerfully, "Night, Pete. See you in the morning."

"Yeah, night, guys. Sleep well."

They held hands as they hurried up the stairs. As Nick pushed open their bedroom door Jackson's heart was pounding hard, and not just because of the two flights they'd climbed. The moment Nick shut the door behind them he put one hand on Jackson's cheek and held his gaze intently. "Can I kiss you?"

Not trusting his voice, Jackson nodded.

Nick moved closer, pressing their bodies together, and Jackson leant into him, closing his eyes as their lips touched and slowly parted as the kiss deepened. Nick tasted of red wine and chocolate, the flavours as decadent as the slow erotic flicker of his tongue against Jackson's. The rest of the world faded away as arousal wound around them, binding them together, and stripping Jackson of reason and logic. The whys and what ifs didn't matter in this intimate space. He put his arms around Nick and held him close, kissing him more deeply as he lost himself in pure sensation.

Nick's hand was under his shirt, resting warm against his chest. Jackson moved his hands down, cupping Nick's gorgeous arse and squeezing.

How often had he imagined doing this? Way too many times. It was easy to imagine, because fortunately—or unfortunately perhaps—Jackson was all too familiar with the contours of Nick's arse. In his club dancing days, he'd worn nothing but a jock, so Jackson had had ample opportunity to admire it when he'd been lucky enough to get a position near the stage. And nowadays, Nick was prone to wandering around the flat in his underwear so Jackson still got to ogle it on a regular basis.

Nick's arse felt as good as it looked, but in Jackson's

imagination, there had always been fewer clothes in the way. With a heady rush, he suddenly realised there was nothing stopping him from getting into Nick's pants... literally. He started working on Nick's fly, breaking the kiss briefly to mutter, "Is this okay?"

"Yeah," Nick said breathlessly.

Once he'd undone Nick's fly, Jackson slipped one hand down the back of his underwear. He groaned as he made contact with the warm curve of Nick's arse. Kissing Nick's neck instead of his mouth, he pushed his fingers into the heat of Nick's crack. "God, that feels good," he muttered.

Nick laughed. "It should be me saying that. *Oh!*" he gasped as Jackson pressed more insistently. "Wow. You're such an arse man, going straight for the hole without so much as a dick squeeze."

"Sorry." Jackson flushed, withdrawing his hand a little. "Your arse is very distracting. Tell me what you want, Nick. I'm up for anything."

"No need to apologise. I'm happy that my arse is such a distraction." He grabbed Jackson's wrist and lifted his hand. Opening his mouth, he sucked on Jackson's middle finger for a moment. "Now carry on," he said with a grin. "And kiss me some more."

Happy to oblige, Jackson pressed his mouth to Nick's while he felt for Nick's hole with his wet finger. Nick adjusted his stance a little, widening his legs to give Jackson access, and they moaned in unison as the tip of Jackson's finger slipped past resistance into the heat of Nick's body.

They carried on kissing, grinding together and Jackson could feel Nick growing hard against him. After a little while Nick broke away and asked, "Will you use your mouth on me instead?"

"On your arse?"

"Yeah, if you're into that? You said you were up for whatever."

"Fuck yes. I'm into that." Into that was an understatement. Licking Nick's arse was the stuff Jackson's most shameful and secret fantasies had been made of for the last several months.

"Brilliant. Let's get naked first." Wriggling out of Jackson's arms, Nick started undressing, tossing his clothes aside carelessly. Jackson followed suit, stripping until the floor was littered with garments and they had nothing left on. They stood there for a moment, both taking a good look. It was so weird standing there opposite Nick, stark naked with their boners pointing at each other.

"I can hardly believe this is actually happening," Jackson said.

"Me neither." There was a pause, then Nick blurted out, "You look so fucking good. All that time at the gym really shows."

"Thanks."

"Nice cock too. I didn't really get a good look at it earlier. I was too busy cramming it into my mouth."

Jackson laughed. "Glad you approve. You look great too." He let his gaze slide appreciatively over Nick. "Turn around so I can see your arse." He gestured with a spinning finger.

"Ooh. Bossy. I like it." Nick spun around obediently, looking over his shoulder as he swayed his hips at Jackson. "So? Is it satisfactory?"

"I'd say it exceeds expectations. In fact, it looks good enough to eat."

"Well that's handy." Nick crawled onto the bed and dropped his head onto his arms, leaving his butt sticking up, legs spread slightly. "Get on with it then."

Jackson smiled as he joined Nick on the bed. Apparently he wasn't the only one who could be bossy. Knowing Nick as well as he did, this was no surprise. Wasting no time, he parted Nick's cheeks and licked over his hole with a firm stroke of his tongue.

"Fuck." Nick's body tensed.

Jackson licked again and then focused his attention where they both wanted it, moving his tongue in gentle circles.

Nick moaned loudly. "Oh Jesus."

"Shhhh." Jackson drew away. "Keep it down. Your parents are downstairs, remember?" He did it again, using a little more pressure now. When he pushed the tip of his tongue in deeper and wiggled it, Nick made a desperate groaning sound. Although there was a fierce satisfaction in hearing Nick do that because of him, he didn't want anyone else to hear it, so he drew back again.

"Don't stop. *Please*, Jackson."

"Seriously, Nick. Keep it down. Pete might be on his way up soon and he doesn't need to hear you braying like a donkey."

"I'm not braying."

"Whatever. Just shush."

"Okay, okay. I'll try." Nick grabbed a pillow and buried his face in it while Jackson started rimming him again. Nick didn't manage to keep quiet, but at least his sounds were muffled now. Jackson reached between Nick's legs and cupped and squeezed his balls, and then he circled his hand around Nick's cock and started stroking him. The noises Nick was making changed pitch a little, increasing in frequency. Jackson wasn't surprised when he surfaced and gasped. "I'm getting pretty close. Do you want me to come like this? Cause if not, you'd better stop."

"Do *you* want to come like this?"

"Ideally I'd like to come with your cock in my arse, but unless you packed any lube and condoms that's not really an option."

The idea planted in Jackson's head took root. He wanted to fuck Nick so badly. "We don't need condoms," Jackson said. "Neither of us have had sex for ages, remember?"

"True. But lube then. My butthole isn't used to having things shoved in it, and your cock's not exactly small. I haven't got anything useful we could use. I don't think toothpaste or hair product will cut it, so unless you have anything better?"

"No, fuck. I wish I did."

"Me too. Tomorrow maybe? We could go and find a petrol station shop for emergency sex supplies."

"Sounds good." The idea of sliding his cock into Nick's arse made Jackson feel almost dizzy with desire.

"For now... I want something in my arse. Will you finger me while you jerk me off? Or you could blow me again? That'll be less messy."

"Of course. Roll over." He slapped Nick lightly on the arse.

Nick lay on his back with his knees bent up and

Jackson settled between them. As he slid a finger into Nick, he stroked Nick's cock with his other hand. Nick gave a gasp of pleasure, and Jackson smiled. With his cheeks flushed and eyes dark and glittering, Nick was so gorgeous. Jackson still couldn't quite believe they were doing this.

"Suck me!" There was an edge of desperation in Nick's voice.

Jackson took Nick in his mouth and drew him deep as he curled his finger, thrusting it carefully in and out.

"Oh fuck, yeah. Don't stop." Nick's body tightened, thighs squeezing Jackson's shoulders. It was a matter of moments before he gave a strangled moan and his hips jerked with the first shot of come. "Fuck," he muttered again, hands finding Jackson's head and holding him there for a few more seconds until he was done. "Wow." His body softened and he released Jackson, saying, "Shit. Was I really loud? I was so out of it I don't even know."

"Nah. You weren't too bad." Jackson knelt between Nick's legs, relieved to be able to get a hand on his own dick at last.

Nick's gaze dropped, eyeing Jackson's cock hungrily. "Man. I wish you could fuck me. But at least I can return the favour. Just give me a minute for my limbs to stop feeling like wet noodles.

"I could fuck your mouth," Jackson suggested. "Then you don't need to move."

Nick's eyes lit up. "Yeah? Sounds good to me. And I think it's your turn to do that anyway. Go for it."

Sprawled back against the pillows, he grinned at Jackson, lips pink and inviting.

Jackson straddled Nick's face, one hand gripping the

headboard as he guided the tip of his cock and rubbed it over Nick's lips, making them wet and sticky. "Open up." He pushed, and Nick opened obediently.

Both hands on the headboard, Jackson began to move his hips carefully, testing to see how much Nick could handle.

Nick made a sound of encouragement. He grabbed Jackson's arse, digging his fingers in and encouraging Jackson to give him more. As Jackson's cock hit the back of his throat he grunted, but didn't try to stop him from moving.

Jackson bit back a groan as he remembered they had to be quiet. He clamped his mouth shut and gritted his teeth, fighting to contain the sounds that wanted to break free as he thrust slowly in and out. The swirl of Nick's tongue and the suction of his mouth felt incredible, but it was the sight of him that was almost too much to bear. Cheeks pink and with an adorable frown of concentration on his brow, Nick's gaze was fixed on Jackson. There was an intensity in his eyes that made it impossible for Jackson to look away.

Although he was the one in the dominant position, he felt utterly powerless. Nick was the one guiding his movements, coaxing him to the brink and keeping him there by slowing down just as Jackson was about to come.

"Nick, please!" he hissed as Nick put the flat of one hand against Jackson's hips, holding him away so he could lick the tip, torturing Jackson with featherlight strokes of his tongue.

"What?" Nick asked, all innocence.

"You're killing me." Jackson's cock jerked.

Nick licked off the precome that escaped, still only

using his tongue and not sucking properly. But it was enough to push Jackson that little bit closer.

"Do you want me to come all over your face?" he asked desperately. "Because if you don't stop teasing me, it's going to happen."

"Yeah?" Nick grinned. "That sounds pretty fucking hot actually." He wrapped his hand around Jackson and started to jerk him off, saying, "Do it!"

Most of Jackson's fantasies about Nick had involved Nick's arse. But as he stroked his cock and gazed at Nick's upturned face he wondered why he hadn't imagined this, because holy shit this was so fucking hot.

"Gonna come," he managed, but his warning was a little late because the first shot splashed right across Nick's cheek and into one eye, making him flinch.

"Shit. Sorry." Jackson aimed lower, getting Nick's lips and chin with the next lot before the final feeble spurt trickled over his own fist.

"Ow!" Eyes shut, Nick scrunched his face up in discomfort. "That stings like a bitch. Quick! Get me a tissue or something."

Jackson looked around helplessly. There were no tissues anywhere that he could see. He leapt up and grabbed his underwear off the floor and wiped his hands on them, before picking up Nick's and bringing them to the bed. "Here." He pressed them into Nick's hand. "Better than nothing."

"Thanks." Nick wiped his face and then cranked his eyes open to see what he was holding and laughed. "Nice."

"First thing I could think of. Are you okay?" He peered at Nick whose eye looked red and sore.

"Just about. I'd better go and rinse it though." He got up and pulled on his jeans before letting himself out of their room.

While he was gone, Jackson put on some clean underwear and then checked the bed. Luckily there was only a tiny wet spot on one of the pillows, which wouldn't be noticeable once it was dry.

Nick returned smelling of toothpaste. He smiled ruefully at Jackson, one eye noticeably red and bloodshot. "Been a while since anyone got me in the eye. I'd forgotten the hazards of facials."

"Let me see." Jackson beckoned for him to sit down on the bed. He put his hand on Nick's cheek and tilted his face towards the light. "Oh shit. I'm really sorry. That looks sore."

"Don't worry about it. It was my own fault. I asked for it."

Jackson chuckled. "Yeah. I guess you did."

They smiled at each other and Jackson's heart swelled. But even as he felt the rush of affection for Nick it was doused by a cold trickle of anxiety. How were they ever going to get back to their old version of normal, when laughing about him coming all over Nick's face didn't feel odd at all?

TEN

Nick lay awake listening to the sound of Jackson's breathing. Deep, slow, and regular, it sounded as though Jackson was asleep but Nick wasn't sure. He thought about asking, but decided not to risk waking him.

Craving comfort, he rolled onto his side and hugged his pillow. He wished he could snuggle up to Jackson, but he didn't know whether that was a good idea. Everything between them was different—temporarily at least—but he wasn't sure exactly what the new boundaries were.

As the post-sex high wore off, Nick felt more and more anxious.

What the fuck were we thinking?

But the *we* was hardly fair, because in his heart Nick knew that nothing would have happened if he hadn't initiated it. Sure, Jackson had been a willing partner in what had followed, but Nick had lit the fuse. This was all down to him.

What the fuck was I thinking?

Thinking hadn't really come into it. When he'd kissed

Jackson in the Pirate Tree earlier, he'd acted on pure instinct. He had no idea where the desire that had swept over him had come from. As long as he'd known Jackson, he'd never wanted him like that before. It wasn't that Jackson wasn't attractive. He was clearly drop-dead gorgeous. But he was also Nick's best friend, his flatmate, his rock. Plus, he wasn't the sort of guy that Nick usually went for. He was far too nice. Jackson was worth a hundred of the arseholes who Nick usually dated. He'd let himself fall for wankers over and over again until he'd finally given up on relationships altogether to focus on himself.

Two years of counselling later, Nick understood what had kept him trapped in that painful cycle of disappointment and heartbreak, and his counsellor thought he was ready to move on. But Nick didn't trust himself. He was still too wary to try again in case he got swept back into that harmful pattern.

If I was in a relationship with Jackson, it would be completely different.

Nick shoved the thought away quickly, because it was too dangerous to think of Jackson like that. Even if Jackson did have feelings for him, who was to say that would last? And if they became lovers, what if Nick got bored and wanted out after a couple of weeks—like he always had with guys who didn't treat him like crap?

All those years of friendship and loyalty could be damaged irrevocably if they risked a relationship and it didn't work out. There was far too much to lose. Somehow they had to find a way to get back to normal once they got home.

One more night, Nick promised himself. *We can have*

just one more night, and then it will be over and everything will go back to how it was.

NICK WOKE to the creak of the bed as Jackson climbed out of it.

"What time is it?"

"Nearly nine," Jackson replied. "I've been awake reading for a while, but I'm getting hungry. I thought I'd have a shower now if that's okay?"

"Yeah. Course. Go for it."

Left alone, Nick got up just long enough to open the curtains and wrinkle his nose at the slate grey sky and the rain. He fell back into bed and watched raindrops trickle down the window pane, hoping the half-arsed daylight would wake his brain up a bit. He was groggy and headachy this morning after tossing and turning for hours last night, stressing about Jackson.

Jackson didn't seem to have had any trouble sleeping, Nick thought resentfully. Why was he the only one losing sleep over this?

Despite his uneasy thoughts, his eyelids drooped and he dozed off again, waking when Jackson returned with a towel around his waist.

"Hey, sleepyhead." He pulled off the towel and threw it at Nick.

"Oi!" Nick sat up and whipped Jackson's arse with the towel until Jackson grabbed it and won the ensuing tug-of-war.

They grinned at each other, and Nick's spirits lifted.

Things were going to be okay. This was Jackson. They'd been mates for too long to fuck this up.

"You getting up, lazy butt?" Jackson asked once he was dressed. "Or am I gonna have to go and forage for breakfast in your parents' kitchen all alone?"

"I'll get up." Nick heaved himself out of bed, stretched and yawned, then started to put on his clothes.

THE RAIN PERSISTED ALL MORNING, and nobody fancied venturing out. Pete took up residence in front of the TV, Nick's dad disappeared into his study, and his mum shut herself away to do some yoga. Nick and Jackson spent the morning helping Maria and Adrian entertain Seth, and helped Nick's mum make lunch while Seth had a short nap.

The early part of the afternoon was more of the same. Nick was bored and restless, glad of the distraction when Seth was around. It was hard to be anxious when his nephew was so cute. He seemed to have decided Nick was his favourite person today, and made Nick read the animal book with him over and over until he got overexcited and boisterous, climbing over Nick and Jackson until they made a pile of cushions for him in the middle of the floor to climb on instead.

Finally he wore himself out and it was naptime again.

"Wave bye to Uncle Nick," Adrian said. "Bye bye." He waved at Nick, demonstrating.

Nick waved back, grinning at Seth. "Bye, Seth. Have a good nap."

Seth blinked, eyes slightly glazed, and then held out a

chubby hand with starfish fingers and opened and closed his fist a few times.

"Clever boy!" Maria beamed from her spot on the sofa. "And wave to Uncle Jackson too."

Nick's heart picked up and he glanced at Jackson. Jackson just smiled and waved to Seth, who mirrored the action again.

Once they'd gone, Nick's gaze strayed to the window. The rain was still falling hard, but he couldn't bear the thought of sitting around for the rest of the day. Then suddenly he remembered there was a very good reason for him to go out.

Standing, he said, "I'm going to pop out to fill the car up with petrol. It was running pretty low when we got here."

"Can't you do it on the way home tomorrow?" Jackson asked, brow furrowed.

"I could. But I fancy getting out. Plus there's a shop at the petrol station." Nick gave him a meaningful look for a second before adding, "And I'm craving some salt and vinegar crisps. Mum and Dad don't have any."

"Really?" Jackson sounded unconvinced.

Had he forgotten what they'd said last night? "Yes. *Really.*" Nick held Jackson's gaze, eyebrows raised meaningfully.

Finally comprehension dawned on Jackson's face. "Oh. Right." He flashed Nick a quick smile, which filled Nick with relief. "Yeah, good idea."

Maria gave them both a strange look and then said, "I might come along too. We're almost out of baby wipes."

"I can pick some up for you," Nick said swiftly. The last thing he needed was company for this mission.

"No. I'll come. I've got cabin fever, and with the weather like this it's my only chance to get out of the house today."

Damn. Nick couldn't think of a good reason to try to talk her out of it. "Okay. You ready to head out now?"

"Yep. Let's go."

How the hell was Nick going to buy lube without her noticing? He shot Jackson a panicked look, and Jackson shrugged and mouthed, "Good luck!"

Luck did seem to be on Nick's side at first, because when they got to the petrol station Maria went ahead into the shop while Nick filled his car with fuel. Hopefully she'd have found what she needed and finished paying by the time he got inside. But when Nick entered she was still browsing in the chocolate aisle.

"Did you find the baby wipes yet?" he asked.

"No. I got distracted." She grinned. "I know I shouldn't give in to temptation after the amount I ate yesterday, but I really fancy some Cadbury's Fruit & Nut."

"Go for it. January is the time for self-control. I always think this week between Christmas and New Year is like a kind of food amnesty. Eat whatever the fuck you like, because it doesn't count."

She laughed. "If only that last part were true. But, you're right about the rest. Fuck it. I'm buying some." She picked up a large bar. "Okay. That's it. No more snacks. I'm going to go and find the baby wipes."

"Take the car keys if you want, then you can let yourself in and wait for me."

"No, it's okay. You won't be long if you're only buying crisps. Look." She pointed. "They're right behind you."

Nick turned and sure enough there they were. The salt and vinegar he'd said he wanted were right at eye level, giving him no excuses. He took a couple of packets off the shelves. "I might see what other snacky stuff they've got," he said vaguely. "Maybe buy some things for the drive tomorrow."

"Okay." Finally she wandered off.

Nick skulked in the snack food aisle, surreptitiously eyeing his sister until he saw her head for the tills. Then he hurried around towards the aisle she'd just left. Baby wipes fell into the general category of health/toiletries that might include lube. He scanned the shelves, finding tissues, pain medications, hand sanitiser, soap.... Then his heart leapt in excitement as he spotted condoms on the top shelf. They had lubricated condoms, but no actual lube.

"Bollocks," he muttered, picking up a packet anyway. They might be better than nothing in a pinch, but Nick preferred a smoother ride. Who the hell made these decisions about what to stock in a shop that supposedly offered essential items? If condoms were essential but not lube it must clearly be some straight bloke who'd never been fucked in the arse. Now Nick would have to find some excuse to drag Maria to a supermarket. At least it was early enough in the afternoon that one would be open, even on Boxing Day.

When he reached the till, Maria was waiting near the door, far enough away not to notice the box of condoms he slipped next to the bags of crisps. He pocketed them as soon as the lady at the till had scanned them, and then he got out his card to pay.

"Did you find everything you were looking for?" she asked with casual disinterest as he tapped in his PIN.

"No," Nick replied. Still annoyed at his thwarted attempt. "I was looking for lube, but you don't seem to sell it."

"Yeah we do. It's on those shelves on the back wall." She pointed.

"Oh. Right." Surprised, Nick took his card back. It would have been more helpful if they'd had this conversation before he'd paid for everything else. "I'll go and look again. Thanks."

"You're welcome, love."

Relieved that his mission was almost accomplished, Nick headed to the far end of the shop. As he rounded the corner he stopped short, staring a shelf full of assorted lubricants—but not the sort that would be any use to him and Jackson. WD40 might be useful for many things, but there was no way Nick was putting it anywhere near his arsehole, the same went for engine oil.

"For fuck's sake! This is no bloody help!"

"Nick. What's up?" Nick whipped around to see Maria standing just behind him. "What are you looking for?"

His cheeks burnt hot as his mouth fell open, but no useful explanation came to mind. "Um." He swallowed. "Nothing. It doesn't matter."

"Is there something wrong with your car?"

"No. Nothing like that. Don't worry about it. Let's just head home." Maybe he could sneak out again later without anyone noticing.

"Why are you being so weird?"

"I'm not being weird." He walked away with Maria on his heels.

"You really are."

He unlocked the car and got behind the wheel. As he started the engine he knew Maria was watching him.

"Nick, what the hell is going on with you today?" she asked.

Fuck it. If he confessed, then he could just go and buy some bloody lube, and then Jackson could fuck him tonight. That was enough motivation to deal with the awkwardness.

He turned to face her. "I was trying to buy lube, but they didn't have any. Well... not the sort I needed anyway. Hence my frustration."

"Lube?" She narrowed her eyes.

"Yes. Lube. Personal lubricant. Intimate lubricant... whatever the fuck they call the type that doesn't go in your car."

"But I thought you and Jackson were only pretending?"

"We are! I mean... we were. Look. I don't know exactly what we're doing, but we need lube, okay? So I'm going to go to Tesco. They'll be open during the day today, and they'll definitely have some there."

"Okay."

Nick put the car in gear and started to drive. The big Tesco store wasn't far, and neither of them spoke on the way there. Nick parked and left Maria in the car. "I won't be long. Do you need anything?"

"No. I'm good, thanks." She gave him a thin smile.

The lube was nice and easy to find in the supermarket. They actually offered quite a selection, but Nick bypassed the stuff that tingled or tasted of strawberries for something more traditional. He paid at the self-service checkout, and the bottle was small enough to fit in his pocket along with the condoms.

When Nick got back to the car, Maria waited till he'd started to drive back before asking tentatively, "When did things change between you and Jackson?"

"Yesterday."

She was silent for a moment. Nick gripped the wheel more tightly and kept his gaze on the road. The light was starting to fade now and the rain was still hammering on the windscreen.

"Oh right. So... I guess it's too soon to tell whether it's going to be an ongoing thing?"

"Yep." Nick could already tell from her doubtful tone what she was thinking, and he didn't want to hear it. "Anyway, we're nearly back now, so can you just drop it?" He sounded defensive and brittle, but that was exactly how he felt.

"Jesus, Nick. I didn't even say anything much."

"Yeah, well. I don't want to talk about it."

"Fine," she snapped back at him, but there was an edge of hurt to her tone.

Nick sighed.

"I'm sorry." He glanced sideways. Maria sat hunched in the passenger seat, her face unhappy. "I didn't mean to be an arsehole about it. It's just that I know what you were going to say, and you're probably right. Getting involved with Jackson would be a daft idea. But it's nothing really. We're just...." He waved one hand vaguely as he searched for the right words. "Having some fun together. It's never going to be anything serious, and I'm pretty sure both of us know that. So where's the harm?"

"How do you know that?"

"Know what?"

"That it's never going to be anything serious? Why couldn't it be serious? You guys are so close already. It could be amazing."

That wasn't what Nick had been expecting her to say at all.

"So you don't think I'm an idiot?"

"I didn't say that. Don't get carried away." She snorted. Then her voice turned serious. "I don't think *getting involved* with Jackson is a terrible idea, but messing around with him sounds dangerous. There's way too much potential for things to get complicated if you aren't both totally clear about what you want. So if you think you're just going to have a bit of fun with Jackson and it's not going to change anything, then you *are* an idiot."

Nick's stomach lurched at the truth of her words. "Yeah. Fair enough." He had no good comeback because he knew she was right. It was too late, though. This thing with Jackson had already been set in motion and things were going to change whether he wanted them to or not. So he figured he might as well see it through. "We'll work it out, I'm sure."

"I hope so. But, Nick, for what it's worth, I think you guys would make a fantastic couple. I always wondered why you weren't together."

"I never thought of him like that before now," Nick admitted. "He was just... Jackson. My friend. The person who picked me up off the floor when someone else dumped me, or cheated on me, or otherwise made me feel like shite. I never thought he wanted more than friendship either. Do you really think he does?"

She laughed. "Nick. If you're buying lube, I think that's a pretty clear indication that both of you are interested in more than friendship."

"But how much more?" Nick's head was whirling with possibilities, shiny and exciting but terrifying too. He wasn't sure whether he wanted to grab them and hang on to them, or turn and flee in the opposite direction.

"You'd have to ask Jackson that."

"Yes. I guess I would."

He'd also need to do some soul-searching of his own.

MARIA'S WORDS stayed with Nick, echoing through his thoughts for the rest of the day in a warning to be cautious, but also stirring up a vague, unformed sense of possibility. Might Jackson really want to be in an actual honest-to-God relationship with Nick? And if that was on offer, did Nick want that too?

On the sofa after dinner, Jackson put his arm casually around Nick's shoulders and Nick leant into his warmth and solidity. He let his mind drift, trying to imagine what their life would look like if they were in a relationship. What would it be like cohabiting as a couple, rather than as friends? What would it be like sleeping with Jackson every night and waking up together? What would it be like to be with someone he trusted, someone who loved him uncondi-tionally, someone he knew back-to-front and inside out and who he felt utterly safe and comfortable with?

Do I want that?

His heart leapt at the thought, swelling with the joyful rightness of it. But Nick tried to squash that emotion down. He didn't dare let himself want too much in case Jackson didn't feel the same. *Maybe.* That was as much as he was prepared to admit.

As bedtime approached, anticipation rose, making Nick's belly flutter and his heart skip faster. Were they going to go through with this? Would Jackson still want to? Should Nick let it happen if he did?

Finally, unable to bear the waiting, he faked a huge yawn.

"I'm going to have to go to bed. I'm shattered."

"What time are you leaving tomorrow?" his mum asked.

"We hadn't really thought yet." He looked at Jackson questioningly and got a shrug in return. "We don't want to get back too late, and I'd rather drive in daylight, so late morning maybe? Or after lunch if you're okay to feed us before we leave."

"Yes, stay for lunch," his dad said. "It won't be anything fancy tomorrow, mostly leftovers probably. But don't rush off early unless you need to."

"Okay, thanks." Nick smiled. "Right. It's bedtime for me anyway. Are you coming, babe?" He patted Jackson's thigh.

"Yeah. I'm tired too."

Nick didn't believe Jackson was either. On the way upstairs he wondered again whether he should try to talk to Jackson before they waded in any deeper.

Once the bedroom door was closed behind them, Nick

turned to face him, heart beating double time. He hesitated, wanting to check in with Jackson and ask how he was feeling, but before he could get any words out Jackson pulled him close and kissed him soundly.

"God. I've been wanting to do that all day."

His smile was so warm and sweet that Nick had to kiss him again.

Fuck talking.

Kissing was so much easier. Body language was pure and uncomplicated in comparison to words. As they held each other close their bodies communicated in unspoken ways that left no room for misunderstanding. Nick might not know what Jackson wanted, or what he himself wanted to happen tomorrow, or next week, or next month. But it was blindingly obvious what both of them wanted in that moment. Desire swept through him in a raging torrent, washing away all his doubts and uncertainties, and Nick stopped fighting and gave himself up to it, letting it carry him inexorably along.

When they finally drew apart again, breathless and smiling, Jackson asked, "Did you manage to get some lube earlier? I never got a chance to ask you." He raised his eyebrows, a hopeful grin on his face. "Please say you did!"

Nick's heart started beating double time. "Yeah. I did."

Jackson seemed to pick up on his anxiety. His expression became serious and he held Nick's gaze as he said quietly, "Are you sure you want to do this? We don't have to if you've changed your mind."

This was Nick's last chance to put the brakes on, to question what they were doing and to find out what Jackson was thinking before he let this happen.

I don't want to know, not yet.

In that moment, Nick wanted Jackson to fuck him more than he wanted anything, and this might be his only chance to have that. If he confessed to possibly-maybe-probably having feelings for Jackson and Jackson *didn't* feel the same, there was no way he'd get fucked tonight. Only a total wanker would use their best friend like that, and Jackson would never do that to Nick. Therefore, according to Nick's hormone-fuelled reasoning, it was better to put that conversation on hold.

"Yes," Nick said. "I'm sure." He took Jackson's hands and led him to the bed.

They undressed between kisses, hands exploring bare skin. The air of the room was cool so they got under the covers, cocooned in warmth as they pressed their bodies together. Lying on his side facing Jackson, Nick could feel the hardness of Jackson's dick. He wrapped a hand around it and stroked. "I can't wait to feel this inside me."

"I can't wait to put it inside you." Jackson's voice was low and intimate and his sexy smile made Nick's toes curl with anticipation. "Where's that lube, baby? Gonna let me get you ready?"

The sound of the endearment sent wild hope fizzing through Nick's veins like champagne. There was nobody else here to overhear them and nothing to prove, so that was all for Nick. Even if it slipped out without Jackson noticing, it must mean something.

"Yeah. I put it in the drawer by the bed. Let me get it." He twisted away to open the drawer. "I got condoms too. I know we don't really need them, but it'll be less messy if we use one."

Jackson chuckled. "Good thinking. Easy clean-up is always good in someone else's house." He took the lube from Nick's hand and pushed him gently onto his back. "Allow me." Jackson moved between Nick's legs, pushing the covers down as he knelt over him. He looked huge from this angle, his powerful shoulders wide and strong, cock jutting out. "Are you warm enough?"

The air was chilly, but it felt good on Nick's skin, tightening his nipples and making his skin more sensitive. "Yeah. I'm fine." He spread his legs a little wider and reached for his dick, teasing it with a gentle grip as he watched Jackson fumble with the seal on the lube.

He turned the bottle around, picking at it with increasing frustration. "For fuck's sake!" he exclaimed. "How am I supposed to get into the bloody thing?"

"Shhh!" Nick cautioned, chuckling. "We need to be quiet, remember? Give it to me... there you go."

Jackson squeezed a generous blob of lube onto his fingertips and rubbed it over Nick's hole. "Jesus! That's cold!"

"Now who's being too noisy?" Jackson grinned wickedly and then pushed his fingers inside, making Nick gasp with the sudden stretch.

"Fuck!"

"Okay?"

"Yeah. You just took me by surprise." Nick stroked his dick, the pleasurable sensation helping to ease the tight pressure.

"Really? What did you think was about to happen?" Jackson teased.

Nick's body was adjusting, the initial discomfort

melting away as Jackson moved his fingers gently in and out. Arousal built fast, curling through him and flushing his skin. "A little warning is nice."

"Sorry." Jackson pushed them a little deeper, curling them just right as he carried on thrusting. His dark eyes were fixed on Nick, watching every reaction.

Nick drew in a shaky breath, hand tightening on his cock. "Oh God. Yeah. That's good." The sensation of urgency that preceded orgasm was already growing. "Just keep it nice and slow."

"Is it too much?"

"No." Nick grinned, breathless. "Well... not in the way you mean. It's too fucking good."

"Do you want my cock instead?" His voice was deep and husky and his gaze so intense Nick couldn't look away.

"Yes."

The wait was almost unbearable as Jackson rolled on a condom. Aching, desperate to be filled again, Nick stroked himself while he watched. His heart was beating so hard he could feel it everywhere in his body, a pulsing drumbeat of anticipation.

"You wanna stay on your back?" Jackson asked.

Nick's mind briefly flashed through a range of possibilities, like porn on fast forward, and settled back to where they were now. "Yeah." He reached for Jackson, guiding him down. If they were only going to do this once, then like this was perfect. This way he could see Jackson's face and watch every shifting expression as they fucked. He could hold him in his arms and kiss him.

He could imagine what it might be like to love Jackson and be loved back.

On second thoughts doing it in this position was terrifying. It would mean pure, raw vulnerability with no place for Nick to hide the confusing mess of feelings that were swirling inside him. But as Jackson eased his cock inside it was already too late. Nick clung to Jackson and moaned, swept away on a rising tide of desire as their bodies began to move together in a dance of intimacy as old as time itself.

They fell into a rhythm as natural as breathing, heat building where skin touched skin. Jackson dipped his head and kissed Nick's shoulder, his neck, his cheek, before finding his mouth. The kiss was long, deliberate, and perilously sweet. Nick flexed his hips to meet each hard thrust of Jackson's cock.

I can't believe we're doing this. The words repeated a loop in his head. How had all those years of friendship led to this?

Jackson started fucking him harder, and the bed creaked in protest.

Nick broke the kiss to whisper, "Slow down. Unless you want people to hear us."

"Fuck," Jackson muttered, breath hot on Nick's cheek. "Okay. I'll try." He took his weight on his arms, putting some space between their torsos. His gaze raked over Nick, hot and possessive, sending a thrilling surge of excitement through Nick. "I can't believe we're doing this."

Nick laughed. "I know. I was just thinking the exact same thing. But we are." He squeezed his muscles around Jackson as if to emphasise his point, and Jackson groaned.

"Damn. You feel good."

"So do you. Come on, keep moving. Just do it slowly so nobody will hear."

Jackson started to fuck him again, rocking into Nick slowly. Each slide of his cock felt deeper than the one before, as though he was trying to reach farther inside with each lazy grind of his hips.

"I'm getting close now," Nick whispered.

"Me too. What do you need?"

"Nothing. Just this." Wrapping a hand around his cock again, Nick started to stroke. The tension coiled and built, rising until he couldn't hold on any longer. "Coming," he gasped as he spilt between them, the blinding pleasure loosening his grip on reality for a moment as he bit his lip to stop himself from groaning.

"Oh fuck, Nick," Jackson muttered. "*Fuck.*" He pushed deep, body shuddering a few times as he came before slumping forwards into Nick's embrace.

Breathing hard, they lay there in silence. Nick held him tight, not wanting the moment to end. But Jackson was already softening inside him, and too soon he drew back. "Let me get this condom off."

The wet patch on Nick's stomach felt cold without Jackson there. "I'd better go and clean up." He got up and reached for some clothes to put on. In the aftermath he was already questioning the wisdom of what they'd just done. No longer connected physically, he felt the emotional distance between them keenly. There were way too many things being left unsaid, and Jackson had to realise that too.

"Me too. The condom might have saved one wet patch, but I still got your spunk all over me."

"Not sorry." Nick managed a convincing grin.

Jackson grinned back, but there was a wariness to his expression that only made Nick feel worse.

They used the bathroom together and got ready for bed. Once they got back under the covers, Nick turned out the lamp. Jackson was on his side facing away from Nick. Did that mean he didn't want to cuddle? "I'm chilly." That seemed like a valid excuse. He moved close and fitted his body against Jackson's. "Is this okay?" he asked as he put an arm around him.

"Yeah."

"You make a good bed warmer."

"Thanks... I guess."

There was a long silence. Nick could feel the lift of Jackson's ribs, his breathing gradually slowing. "Are you sleepy?"

"Mmmhmm."

A little later Jackson stirred. "Too hot now," he mumbled, shifting away from Nick.

Nick rolled to lie on his other side and hugged his pillow instead of Jackson. A lump of anxiety sat in his stomach like cold porridge, and it took him a long time to fall asleep.

ELEVEN

Jackson woke with a start from a dream where he was riding a bicycle with no brakes down a mountain, trying desperately to stay on the narrow path. Heart pounding, he took a deep steadying breath as reality asserted itself. But then he became aware of Nick lying beside him and his stomach lurched again as he remembered what they'd done last night.

God....

He let the memory of it flow through his mind, a curl of warm joy and excitement rising in his chest before it was swiftly doused with a bucket of emotions that were far less pleasant: regret, self-reproach, and fear mingled in a cold sweeping tide that wiped out all the good feelings without leaving even a trace behind.

The prospect of returning home today shocked him into the realisation of how stupid he'd been. Maybe Nick could handle them having casual sex, or being friends-with-benefits, or fuck buddies, or whatever people called it. But Jackson knew it wasn't right for him. Being friends with Nick had been manageable before, despite his secret attraction. But now he knew what he was missing, it would be infinitely more difficult.

Sighing, he checked his watch and saw that it was half six. He lay there for a little while, listening to the judgemental voice in his head telling him what an idiot he was, and listing all the ways he'd fucked this up.

There was no way he would be able to get back to sleep with all these thoughts rattling around his head.

One thing Jackson was sure of. If he was going to stand any chance of regaining his equilibrium with Nick, this had to stop right now. They were going to go home today and find a way to put this behind them, write it off as some kind of temporary insanity. If Jackson had his way he'd forget it had ever happened, but failing that, he'd make damn sure it would never happen again.

With that thought in mind, he pushed the covers aside and got out of bed as quietly and carefully as he could. Nick stirred but remained asleep as Jackson fumbled around in the darkness, trying to gather up his clothes so he could get dressed in the bathroom. On his way to the door, he bashed his knee on the corner of the bed with a loud thump and cursed at the sharp pain.

"Jackson?" Nick sat up, a dim shape in the darkness.

"Yeah. Sorry. I didn't mean to wake you."

"What are you doing?"

"Getting up. I was going to go and have a shower."

"What time is it?"

"Six thirty."

"Ugh. Seriously? Why so early? Come back to bed for a bit."

"No. I'm wide awake. And I'm up now. Shh. Go back to sleep." His hand was already on the door handle. Jackson had to escape the delicious temptation of a warm Nick in a cosy bed, because he'd already demonstrated that he couldn't trust himself to behave.

"Are you okay?" Nick's tone had an edge of worry.

"Yeah. Yeah, I'm fine." He knew he didn't sound very convincing, but it was the best he could manage.

Out on the landing with the bedroom door shut behind him, Jackson took a deep breath and blew it out through his mouth slowly, shaking his head.

He was so fucking far from fine.

But he'd get over it—somehow.

NICK GOT up and started packing while Jackson was showering. He'd been hoping for a lie-in, and perhaps a morning blow job. But it seemed that was off the cards. Maybe it was for the best. They should probably use their mouths for talking instead.

When Jackson returned, fully dressed and smelling of shampoo and toothpaste, Nick greeted him with a smile that felt slightly strained.

"You sure you're okay?"

"Yeah. I'm fine." Jackson's answering smile lacked its usual warmth, and he turned away to put his washbag down. But before Nick could ask anything more searching, he added, "I'm hungry though. I think I might head down to get some breakfast, if that's okay?" His gaze raked over

Nick's state of undress. "I'm assuming you want to shower first?"

Nick wasn't sure if he was asking for permission because it was Nick's family home, or whether he was asking if Nick minded Jackson going without him.

"Yeah sure. Help yourself to anything. Mum and Dad won't mind. I'm going to finish packing, then I'll jump in the shower and follow you down in a bit."

"Okay."

Left alone, Nick threw himself back on the bed for a moment and lay staring at the ceiling.

Is he avoiding me?

Maybe he really was hungry, and Nick was just being paranoid. His anxiety about everything was clouding his ability to think clearly. He got up and carried on packing, going through the motions on autopilot while his thoughts ran in unhelpful and unhappy circles.

WHEN NICK WENT DOWNSTAIRS, he followed the sound of conversation to the kitchen and found everyone was there aside from Pete—who was presumably still in bed. Seth was in his highchair eating a piece of toast that had been cut into fingers while the adults sat around the table. Some of them were eating, others drinking cups of tea or coffee.

"Morning, Nick." His dad noticed him first, greeting him with a smile and a nod.

"Good morning, everyone." Nick let his gaze flit around before settling on Jackson. Their eyes locked and Nick's heart did a weird fluttery thing. But then Jackson looked away and the feeling was stamped out by disappointment.

Seeking distraction, Nick focused his attention on Seth who had brown smears all over his face.

"Hey, buddy. What are you eating?"

"Marmite on toast." Adrian wrinkled his nose. "I can't believe any son of mine could like that stuff!"

"He's my son too," Maria said. "He clearly got the loves-Marmite gene from me."

"Well he definitely didn't get it from me! It's vile."

Jackson chuckled, sounding like his normal self. "Ah, the great Marmite debate. I'm with you, man. It's gross."

"Lies. It's delicious!" Nick joined in, relieved. This argument was familiar ground and he latched onto it, glad of the normality.

"Nah," Jackson said. "Your taste buds must be deficient."

Nick's spirits lifted as they grinned at each other. "Bollocks. There's nothing wrong with my taste buds."

"Nick!" his mum said. "Watch your language around Seth!"

"Oh, shit. Sorry," Nick said to Maria and Adrian, and then he clapped his hand over his mouth in horror. "Sorry again!" He grimaced. "Wow. Not swearing is really hard."

"Don't worry. He's heard worse from his car seat," Adrian said. "Especially when his mum's driving."

"Yeah." Maria gave a rueful smile. "I need to work on that. At this rate his first proper word is going to be wanker."

Everyone laughed at that, including Seth.

• • •

A LITTLE LATER, Maria and Adrian announced they were going out for a walk. "Anyone fancy joining us?"

It was dry today, and sun had just broken through the clouds outside. Nick wasn't feeling very energetic, but given that he'd be sitting in a car all afternoon it would probably be nice to get out for a while. "Yeah. I'll come."

"Me too," Jackson said.

"Yes, I'll come," Nick's mum said. "I could do with some fresh air. Reg, what about you?"

"No. There's something I need to get on with this morning."

"Can't it wait? It's lovely outside now."

"No. I want to get it finished."

"Oh. Okay." Her brow furrowed but she didn't press him.

It was muddy after the rain, but the crisp clear air and the scent of wet leaves and earth woke Nick's senses and lifted his spirits a little.

Adrian and Maria led the way. They were holding hands, and Seth was on Adrian's back in a baby carrier. The sight of the three of them opened up an old familiar longing in Nick's heart. During his string of dating disasters, Nick had kept hoping that he'd finally meet the right guy. Someone he could share his life with, someone to grow old with, someone to have a family with. But eventually he'd given up. Being single had seemed a better option than giving pieces of his soul away with every failed relationship.

He glanced at Jackson who was walking beside him, gaze fixed down on the muddy path. Maybe the right guy had been under his nose all along and Nick had been too blind to recognise him. Now he'd broken his addiction to dating wankers, he could imagine being in a relationship with Jackson. If Jackson wanted it too, then Nick really believed it could work. But Jackson had been so distant this morning, it didn't seem likely they were on the same page.

His foot caught on a tree root and he slipped, lurching sideways and grabbing hold of Jackson as he flailed, trying to stay on his feet.

"Whoa. Careful!" Jackson said, clapping an arm around him to keep him upright.

"Sorry." Nick flushed. "I wasn't looking where I was going."

"That was close," his mum said from behind them. "I thought you were going to end up on your back in the mud! Good catch, Jackson."

"Yeah. Thanks." Nick smiled.

"Any time." Jackson lips curved in a faint echo of a smile as he drew his arm away.

Nick felt the loss of contact like a blow. His palm tingled with the urge to take Jackson's hand, but Nick was afraid to risk it. He didn't know what the boundaries were now and was afraid of inadvertently crossing some invisible line he couldn't sense. If only they'd had a chance to talk this morning. He wanted to know what was going on in Jackson's head.

Distracted, he slipped again on a patch of leaves, his heel skidding away from him.

This time Jackson caught his arm. "Blimey, what's going on with you? You're a dancer, you're supposed to be coordinated." His tone was teasing.

"We all have our off days," Nick replied. "I think it may

be a sign I need some new walking boots too. The grips on these have worn right down." He tried to take his arm back, but Jackson kept hold of him.

"Lucky you've got me to help you stay on your feet then." He took Nick's hand and they carried on walking.

"Yeah. Thanks," Nick said, squeezing his hand.

Jackson gave him a quick grin. Bittersweet feelings swirled in Nick's chest, but he did his best to smile back and hide the turmoil inside.

WHEN THEY GOT BACK to the house, Pete was in the kitchen eating a bowl of cornflakes.

"Hello," he said. "I wondered where everyone had got to. I thought you'd all been abducted by aliens or something."

"Your father's in," their mum said. "He's busy with something in his study."

"Who wants tea or coffee?" Maria asked as she filled the kettle.

"Good idea. Tea please." Nick's mum's eyes lit up. "Ooh, I've just remembered there's a lovely tin of biscuits we haven't even started on yet. Let me go and fetch them."

Once they'd made a pot of tea and a pot of coffee, they sat around the kitchen table eating their way through the biscuits. Nick was halfway down his second cup of tea when his dad came in to join them.

"There's tea in the pot if you want some, love," Nick's mum said.

"Thanks. How about the biscuits, are there any left for me?" he asked.

"You'd better get in quickly," Maria replied. "I think we've nearly demolished them."

"Crikey, you have!" He peered into the tin. "I'd forgotten how quickly a tin of biscuits can disappear with all the family home... all the family with some new additions, I should say." He smiled at Adrian and then Jackson.

Nick felt a sudden flash of guilt. Now he'd healed the rift with his dad it felt wrong to have deceived them about the nature of his relationship with Jackson. It was too late now, though. At some point down the line he'd have to make up more lies to explain a separation, or a dissolution of the relationship. That was a depressing thought.

As his dad leant across him to reach the biscuit tin, Nick spotted a smudge of something green on his face. "Dad, you've got paint on your cheek." He pointed.

"Have I?" He drew back, rubbing ineffectually at the smear with his free hand. "Ah well, it's an occupational hazard. I'll get it off later. I only came out to grab a cup of tea and a biscuit or two. I'm going to do a bit more painting before lunch." With that he picked up his tea and headed off again.

"What's he up to?" Maria asked. "He seems to be on a bit of a mission today."

"No idea." Their mum shrugged and then she turned to Nick and asked, "What time do you want to have lunch? I know you and Jackson didn't want to leave too late."

Nick glanced up at the kitchen clock. It was already nearly midday. "In an hour or so? I'd like to try and leave by about half one. But we won't need much lunch. I'm not very hungry after the biscuit frenzy."

"Well there's plenty of bread and cheese for sandwiches, and turkey leftovers of course."

"That sounds perfect."

LUNCH ENDED up being a little later than planned, but by two o'clock Nick and Jackson had packed the car and were ready to say their farewells. Nick's family were assembling in the hall to see them off, Seth was in Maria's arms, fresh from his nap and still looking a little sleepy.

"Will he come to me for a cuddle?" Nick asked.

"Try him. What do you think, Sethie? Got a hug and a kiss for Uncle Nick?"

Nick held out his arms and was rewarded by an adorable smile and a happy noise, so Maria handed him over. Nick kissed Seth's cheek. "Goodbye, buddy. Tell your mum and dad to come and visit us soon." He smiled at Maria. "You know you're always welcome at ours."

"Thanks. We might take you up on that."

"Of course. You must have a spare room in your flat now," Nick's mum said, eyes lighting up. "I'd love to come to London sometime and stay over... if you wouldn't mind putting me up?"

He could hardly refuse. "Um, yeah. Of course." Nick shot Jackson an anxious glance.

"Absolutely." Jackson's tone was unconcerned, but Nick knew him well enough to recognise the tension hiding in the set of his jaw.

Nick always hated the awkwardness of goodbyes, and this was even worse than usual. Keen to get away, he handed Seth back to Maria and gave her a hug and a kiss, and then he moved on to hug Adrian, and then Pete as Jackson followed him down the line of people.

"Where's Dad?" he asked his mum with a frown. "He knows we're leaving, yes?"

"Yes," his mother assured him. "Reg!" she called loudly. "Hurry up, will you?"

"Coming!" His dad's voice came through the study door as it opened. "Sorry to keep you. I just needed to make sure this was dry enough. I think it's okay, but you might want to make sure you pack it where it won't touch anything just in case." He emerged carrying a canvas. "I wanted to give you this," he said to Nick, holding out the painting of the Pirate Tree.

A lump grew in Nick's throat as he studied it. The familiar shape of the trunk and branches, so firmly etched onto his mind's eye, were perfectly depicted there, and the rich green hues of the leaves and the blue of the sky reminded him of countless summer days spent playing in the woods. Three children with hair in varying shades of red and chestnut sat high on the platform, with a black and white pirate flag strung overhead.

"Wow, that's pretty cool, Dad!" Pete's admiring voice broke the silence.

Nick swallowed hard. "Yeah." He managed a dry croak. "Yeah, it's awesome. Thanks, Dad."

"Are you sure?" He ran a hand through his thinning grey hair. "I won't be offended if you don't have space for it in your flat. But I thought maybe...."

"I love it," Nick said firmly. He took the painting and handed it to Jackson and then turned to his dad and drew him into a fierce hug. "I really love it. Thank you."

"You're welcome," his dad muttered into his shoulder. He held tight to Nick for a moment, and when he drew back his eyes were suspiciously bright.

Jackson shook his dad's hand while Nick hugged his mum. "Thanks for having us, Mum, and for persuading me to come."

"Thank you for coming." She squeezed him and kissed his cheek before releasing him. "It's been lovely seeing you—both of you." She smiled at Jackson and opened her arms to hug him too.

"Thanks, Sue," Jackson said.

She addressed Nick directly. "Don't leave it so long next time. Come back soon."

"I will." Nick wanted his parents to be part of his life again, so he made a promise to himself that he would return—with or without Jackson.

His family came outside to wave them off, and Nick watched them in the rear-view mirror, waving out of his window until they were out of sight.

"Well," he said with a sigh of relief. "That went a hell of a lot better than I was expecting."

"Yeah. You and your dad seem to be getting on fine now."

"Mum was right. He really has changed."

"I'm glad you gave him a chance," Jackson said.

"I'm glad too. I probably wouldn't have done without you there to push me, so thank you."

"You're welcome."

Nick glanced across at him. "And thanks again for coming with me."

"You're welcome," Jackson repeated. He didn't meet Nick's gaze.

There was so much more Nick wanted to say, but he didn't know where to begin, and he was too afraid to try in case he fucked it up. Now probably wasn't the best time anyway. Starting a serious conversation in a car was dangerous, because if it went badly there was nowhere to escape.

JACKSON HAD the sense of something slipping away from him as Nick's car ate up the miles, gradually getting them closer to home.

Home.

What was it going to be like being back there? Were they going to be able to put the weirdness behind them and get back to normal?

Nick was driving with his gaze fixed on the road ahead. He'd put on a playlist of music for the drive and his hands were curled tight on the steering wheel as he beat out the rhythm with his thumbs. The tension in the car was painfully obvious, but neither of them seemed ready to try to clear the air.

There was an ache in Jackson's chest and an unsettled antsy feeling in his stomach. He wished he could get to the gym and chase it away by pushing his body until his muscles hurt more than his heart. As it was, he was stuck immobile in a car for three hours with Nick—the source of his current discomfort. It was making him feel a little crazy. When he got home, he could at least go out for a run.

Maybe that would burn off this unbearable sense of longing and frustration.

I'm such a fucking idiot.

Cursing himself once again for getting into this mess, Jackson got out his phone and earbuds. "I'm going to listen to a podcast for a bit."

"Okay."

He selected one of the health podcasts he subscribed to and settled back to listen. It was a welcome distraction and his anxiety slowly settled as he listened to the interview and watched the world flash by the car window. After half an hour or so, his eyelids started to feel heavy, so he closed them and allowed his mind to drift until he dozed off. He slept fitfully, pulled back into consciousness by every small sound as Nick moved, and every *click-click-click* of the indicator as Nick changed lanes.

At some point, Nick's voice brought him back as he asked softly, "Jackson. You asleep?"

Jackson had been asleep until the moment he'd been asked the question, and he wasn't in the mood for conversation anyway, so it seemed easier not to respond. His closed eyes and immobility would answer for him.

TWELVE

When they got home, Jackson went straight to his room to unpack. He could hear the TV in the living area, so he knew Nick must have been out there. Jackson couldn't avoid him forever, but his restless anxiety of earlier had returned full force, so he got into his running kit. Maybe some exercise would help him chill out and deal with everything better.

"Oh, hey," Nick said as Jackson emerged from his room. "I was about to ask if you wanted a tea or coffee, but I guess not."

"Nah. But thanks."

"You heading to the gym?"

"Nope. Just going for a run."

"Okay. Have a good one."

"Cheers."

It was dark outside, but the route Jackson chose was well-lit. He stuck to the side streets so there weren't too many pedestrians to dodge, and when he reached the park he ran laps until his body was exhausted and his mind had calmed.

"You were ages." Nick glanced up from the TV when Jackson got home.

"I was in the mood for a long run after having a break over Christmas."

"Fair enough." Nick's gaze flitted over Jackson in a way that reminded Jackson of being naked with him. "I was thinking of getting a takeaway tonight. We haven't got any decent food till we go shopping. What d'you reckon?"

"Yeah. Sounds good to me."

"What do you fancy? I was leaning towards Chinese or Thai."

"Thai would be my first choice."

"That's fine. I can order while you shower. I'm starving. Do you want your usual?"

"Yes please." Jackson wasn't feeling particularly hungry, maybe the run had dulled his appetite. But he didn't want to keep Nick waiting.

THEY ATE in front of the TV, which Jackson was grateful for. Sitting at the table to eat would have meant the need for conversation. He didn't know how to talk to Nick anymore. His stomach was knotted with nerves and his palms were sweaty like a teenager's on a first date, and it was ridiculous because he was a grown man hanging out with his best mate. It shouldn't have been this difficult.

Jackson was a creature of habit, and he always had prawn red curry with a side of coconut rice. Thai food was his absolute favourite, and he normally ate every scrap, but tonight he picked out all the prawns—he wasn't going to waste those—but left quite a lot of rice and sauce on his plate.

"Is that all you're eating?" Nick asked in surprise as Jackson put his plate on the coffee table.

"Yeah."

"Blimey. That's not like you. Are you sick or something?"

"Nah. I'm fine. Just full." Jackson patted his unhappy stomach. He'd never realised that lovesick was actually a thing, but his lack of appetite seemed to prove it was.

Nick hadn't finished all his food either, but that wasn't unusual for him. He didn't tend to eat quite as much as Jackson, so he often kept some leftovers for the next day when they got takeaway.

Jackson looked across to find Nick was still watching him. There was a small furrow between his brows and his cheeks were flushed.

Nick cleared his throat. "Look. Um. Do you think we should talk about... what happened over Christmas?" His nervous expression didn't give Jackson any useful clues. It could have meant anything from, *It was all a huge mistake and now I feel really awkward*, to *I have feelings for you and I'm freaking out*.

But Nick didn't want a relationship. Hell, he'd told Jackson enough about his counselling for him to know that Nick had basically been in recovery for the past two years and was actively choosing to stay single. So even if by some miracle Nick *did* have feelings for Jackson he probably wasn't happy about that, and he'd be doing his level best to resist them.

How was talking about any of that going to help? Jackson didn't want to hear Nick make some heartfelt speech where he let him down gently. He'd never had any expectations in the first place so there was nothing to say.

"Nah." Jackson desperately tried to keep his voice light and casual. "No need to analyse it. It was just a bit of fun, right?"

"Yeah?" Nick's tone was doubtful. "You sure?"

"Yeah. There's nothing to talk about. Let's just chalk it up to experience and get back to normal. I don't want things to be weird."

"No. No. Me neither." Nick's pink cheeks clashed with his red hair. "So yeah, that's fine. If that's what you want, we'll forget about it and move on. Never speak of it again." As he mimed zipping his lips his grin was a pale shadow of its usual brightness.

"I think that's for the best." Now Jackson could set about gathering the shreds of his pride and pretend that his heart hadn't been split wide open. It would knit together again eventually.

"Right, cool."

There was a painful pause as the television wittered on in the background.

"So, what do you want to do this evening?" Nick's voice was artificially bright, the edges too sharp and brittle to be convincing. "Fancy renting a movie or watching something on Netflix?"

"No." Jackson desperately needed some space from Nick tonight. "I'm pretty tired. I think I'll go to bed and read. Hopefully have an early night." He wanted to be alone to lick his wounds and process everything that had happened. The sooner he got through feeling unhappy and angry with himself, the sooner things could get back to normal.

AS NICK LAY in bed that night there was a strange emptiness inside him. After Jackson had disappeared into his bedroom, Nick had stayed up late and watched two films back-to-back and refused to allow himself to dwell and feel miserable. Given that it was past midnight by the time he'd come to bed, he'd hoped that he wouldn't have any trouble sleeping.

But the peaceful solitude of his bedroom and the comfortable expanse of his king-size bed felt like loneliness tonight. He hugged his pillow close to his chest and stared into the darkness, wide awake, and wondering whether Jackson was losing sleep too.

He sighed and rolled onto his back.

How could things have changed so quickly? Just a few days ago, Nick would never have even imagined having sex with Jackson, let alone being in a relationship with him. Now, those things were all he could think about.

But Jackson had made his position crystal clear.

Just a bit of fun.

Get back to normal.

The words had stung, but at least Nick knew where he stood.

The sound of Jackson's bedroom door opening made Nick's ears prick up. He lay still, listening as Jackson went into the bathroom.

Should Nick have pushed for the conversation Jackson had tried so hard to avoid? It bothered him that he hadn't been honest with Jackson. Maybe it was selfish, but he didn't want Jackson to think that what had happened hadn't meant anything to him, and he didn't believe that Jackson had been totally unmoved by it either. Even if Jackson didn't want to take things further, Nick couldn't have totally imagined the connection between them. It was more than physical. How could it not have been when they'd been best friends long before they'd ever kissed?

He loved Jackson. That wasn't new or shocking. He'd loved Jackson for years with an easy, reciprocal, platonic love that was solid and safe and sure.

But this was something different.

His heart began to race as he allowed this new feeling to unfold in his chest, thrilling and terrifying as it rose, impossible to contain.

I'm in love with him.

"Fuck!" Nick said the word out loud, a release of tension as he stopped fighting the truth. "Fuck, fuck, fuck. What the fuck do I do now?"

The flush of the toilet came, followed by the click of the bathroom door opening and the barely audible pad of Jackson's feet on the carpet as he walked quietly back past Nick's door.

Acting purely on impulse, Nick shot out of bed without stopping to think. He already knew what he had to do as he hurried to Jackson's door. Before he could talk himself out of it, he knocked and waited, heart pounding.

"Yeah?" Jackson's voice came from inside.

"Can I come in?" Nick wished he'd paused long

enough to put on his dressing gown. The heating had gone off for the night and he was chilly in just his boxers and T-shirt.

"Yes."

"Hi." Nick opened the door and slipped inside. He picked his way carefully through the darkness until he found the foot of Jackson's bed. "Is it okay if I sit down?"

"Course. What's up?"

"I want to talk to you."

There was silence.

"Can't it wait till the morning?" Jackson said at last.

"No. It can't."

There was a sigh. "Okay." The bed creaked as Jackson's weight shifted. He switched the bedside lamp on and they both blinked at each other in the sudden glow. Jackson was sitting up against the headboard, and Nick sat at the foot facing him.

His heart lurched painfully as he let his gaze rake over his friend's face. It was so intimately familiar, yet there was a distance between them now that scared him. It was ironic really, how physical intimacy could cause an emotional rift. Surely it was supposed to be the other way around?

This is why I need to be honest.

With a sudden blast of clarity, Nick realised that whatever happened as a result of this conversation it could only make things better. Hiding his feelings from Jackson would drive the wedge between them deeper. If he shared how he felt, even if Jackson didn't want to be with him afterwards, at least everything would be out in the open. Nick would find a way to get over it, and then they could focus on rebuilding their friendship together.

"I think I accidentally fell in love with you," he blurted, the words tumbling over each other in anxious haste.

"You... what?" Jackson's brow furrowed. "Slow down. I didn't—"

"I love you. Not just like a friend." Nick wanted to make sure that Jackson couldn't misunderstand him. This was balls to the wall time and he needed Jackson to get exactly what he was saying. "I've always loved you, but now I'm *in* love with you. I know you probably don't feel the same, and that's okay." It wasn't okay. It wasn't okay at all. But he'd deal. "But I need to tell you, because it matters. And also because I don't like having secrets from you."

He stopped and waited, searching Jackson's face for a reaction. Jackson stared back at him in wide-eyed amazement. He looked as if he'd been electrocuted.

"Okay. I'm done. That was it," Nick said with a shrug. "You're supposed to talk now."

"Um. Yeah. Fuck." Jackson closed his eyes and shook his head as though to clear it. "Sorry." He stared at Nick again. "Am I awake? Because if not, this is a really vivid dream."

"Yes. You're awake!" Frustrated now, Nick leant over and thumped Jackson hard on the leg.

"Ow."

"See. Not a dream." He thumped him again to prove the point.

"Okay, okay! Stop hitting me." Jackson grabbed his wrist and held it tight. He studied Nick as though seeing him for the first time. "Are you sure?"

"Yes. I'm sure."

"Since when?"

Nick hadn't planned this conversation. But if he had, this wouldn't have been how he would have expected it to go. Surely when you declared your love for someone it wasn't supposed to turn into an inquisition.

"Since Christmas."

Jackson's expression was weirdly tense. "You mean since we fucked?"

"Well, technically yes... but it's not just about the sex. I think maybe it's been building for a long time but I never realised before."

Finally, a small smile lifted the corners of Jackson's mouth. "Yeah?" He released his death grip on Nick's wrist.

"Yes," Nick said earnestly, taking his hand. "I already loved you as a friend. I just never imagined anything different between us, and then... Christmas happened." He waved his free hand. "And bam! Suddenly it was all sexual chemistry up the wazoo, and it made me wonder why we hadn't always been doing that. It just seems like we should be together. *Real* boyfriends, not fake ones." Jackson's smile was wider and more sure now, and hope began to swell in Nick's chest like a balloon inflating. "So?" He raised his eyebrows. "You haven't actually told me how you feel about all this?"

It felt as though the whole world stopped for a moment as they gazed into each other's eyes.

Nick could hardly breathe as he waited. He tightened his hold on Jackson's hand, willing him to say what Nick needed so desperately to hear.

When the words came they were soft, slow, and utterly deliberate. "I love you too."

The rush of joy and relief made Nick feel almost dizzy.

"Oh, thank fuck." He put his free hand over his heart, as if reassuring it that it was safe now. "I'm so glad I'm not the only one. Also, I'm fucking freezing. Can I get into bed with you now?"

Jackson grinned. "I think it would be rude not to, at this point."

They both laughed as Nick scrambled under the duvet.

"Come here." Jackson put his hand on Nick's cheek.

They kissed, a sweet soft brush of lips, before Nick snuggled closer, burrowing into Jackson's warmth. "Mmm. This is perfect." He hitched a leg over Jackson's hip and kissed him again, longer and deeper, feeling arousal begin to wake and spread. But then something occurred to him, a piece of the puzzle that hadn't yet slotted into place, and he wanted to know how it fit. "Hey. So how long have you been in love with me?"

Jackson hesitated before answering. "A while."

"How long is 'a while'?"

"I don't know. Like you said, it kind of crept up on me. But looking back... a few months at least, maybe longer. Maybe a lot longer. I had a thing about you when we first met to be honest, and then it got rekindled when I broke up with Tomas and moved in with you. I didn't let myself call it love though. I just knew I had a weird crush on you and it was doing my head in."

Nick frowned. "But why didn't you say anything?" The idea of keeping a secret like that for so long was unimaginable to Nick.

"Because I didn't think there was any chance you felt the same. And even if you did—I knew you didn't want to be in a relationship. You told me enough about your counselling sessions for me to know that was off the table. So what was the point in telling you?"

"I suppose."

"Since we're on the subject." Jackson drew back a little and gave Nick a searching look. "I have to ask. Are you sure about how you feel?"

"Yes!"

"Like, really sure? You're not just infatuated, or in love with the *idea* of being in love like you were with all those other guys?"

Now Nick almost wished he hadn't confided so much in Jackson about the work he'd done with his counsellor. He'd never imagined it was going to come back and bite him on the arse.

"I'm sure. This is totally different. I *know* you, Jackson. I know you back to front and inside out, the good parts and the not-so-good parts. I know you always leave toothpaste dribbles on the side of the sink, and toast crumbs on the counter—but you still get mad at me if I don't empty the bin once in a while. And I know you can be a moody arse-hole after a long day at work and are weirdly possessive about TV remotes."

"All true. But I'm not sure this is helping to convince me about your feelings. Just saying." Jackson grinned.

Nick held his gaze and continued. "And I know you're the most loyal friend a guy could have. I know you always make time to listen to me when I need it, and you bring me cups of tea and sandwiches when I get stuck at my desk because of a deadline. I know you cry every time you watch *The Lion King*. And I know you've got a huge heart."

Jackson's lips quirked. "I thought you were going to say something else there for a minute."

Nick laughed. "Yeah, well. That's pretty big too, but that's not why I love you either. That's just a bonus."

"I think you'll find it's a bon-*er*."

"Is it?" Nick reached down to check. "No it's not. Lies."

"It will be in a minute if you keep squeezing it."

"Awesome. Are we done talking for now?"

"Yeah. I think so."

"Cool. In that case"—Nick started to wriggle down the bed—"I'd like to use my mouth for something else." He pulled Jackson's underwear down and off. "Lie on your back."

Nick settled between his thighs and nuzzled his balls, breathing in the musky scent as Jackson's cock hardened against his cheek. When he finally took it into his mouth, Jackson groaned. He put his hands in Nick's hair. "Feels so good."

"Mmm." It felt good for Nick too. He sucked Jackson deeper, stroking his balls and reaching to rub lightly on the skin behind them.

"Yeah." Jackson spread his legs wider, drawing his knees up in clear invitation.

Nick paused long enough to lick his fingers, before getting back to sucking while he teased Jackson's hole with a wet fingertip.

"Do it!"

A surge of desire lit Nick up like a Christmas tree as he eased his finger inside. Damn. He was tight. Nick knew enough about Jackson's sex life to know that he was almost exclusively a top. The vice-like grip on his finger proved it.

He stopped sucking and used his hand to stroke instead. "Relax. If you want it. Stop fighting it."

Jackson gave a huff of frustration. "I'm trying."

"You got any lube in here? That would help."

"Maybe? Try the bedside drawer."

Nick's rummaging was rewarded as he found a half-full bottle lurking at the back. There were condoms there too; those might come in handy later if Jackson wanted to fuck him again. Then again, Jackson might just want a finger in the butt and a blow job tonight. Nick was okay with that. There would be plenty more opportunities for him to get fucked by Jackson now they'd got their feelings out in the open.

He got back to jerking Jackson off while he worked a finger inside him. The lube helped, and Jackson seemed more relaxed on the second attempt. "Does that feel okay?" Nick asked, curling his finger and rubbing gently.

"It feels amazing actually," Jackson said breathlessly. "Fuck. I'd forgotten how good it feels having something in my arse."

"Reckon you can handle more?"

"Let's find out." A second finger slipped in relatively easily. Jackson tensed for a moment and then relaxed with a groan. "Yeah. That's still good."

After a couple more minutes, Jackson said, "I'm getting pretty close. But I don't want to come yet."

"What do you want to do?"

"Will you fuck me?"

Had Nick heard that right? "Hell, yeah! But... are you sure? I thought you didn't normally—"

"I don't. But yeah, I'm sure. I want you to do it."

"Shit. Okay." Flustered at the surprise request, Nick had a sudden flash of performance anxiety. He let his fingers slip free. "I'll just find a condom. I saw some a minute ago. Hang on."

His hands shook as he tore the wrapper open.

"Nick?" Jackson's voice was soft. "You okay?"

"Yeah.... Bollocks! It's the wrong way around. Gimme a sec." His nerves and the delay meant his erection was flagging a little.

"Slow down. There's no rush. We can do something different if you want."

"No! I want to do this. I just.... I'm a bit nervous that's all." His cheeks heated at the admission. "This all feels like a really big deal... the whole you and me thing, and me topping when I don't do that very often. I'm worried I'll cock it up."

Jackson grinned. "Pun intended?"

Nick gave a burst of anxious laughter and immediately felt a little better. "No. It wasn't actually."

"It will be good," Jackson said. "Even if we cock it up, it will be good because it's you and me. Because it's *us*."

"Okay." Nick took a deep breath and blew away the last of his uncertainty. "Yeah. You're right." He took hold of his cock and started to squeeze and stroke. It didn't take long for him to be back ready for action.

Once he was hard, Jackson took the condom and rolled it on for him. The firm grip of his hand sent a thrill of anticipation rushing through Nick's body.

"You ready?" Nick asked.

"Yeah."

Nick took it very carefully, easing his way in and watching Jackson for any sign of discomfort. "Okay?"

"Yep." The word was clipped, his voice tense, so Nick didn't push any deeper. He waited, letting Jackson adjust to the sensation.

"Keep going," Jackson said.

Nick pushed in all the way. "That's it." He grinned. "Still okay?"

"Yeah." This time Jackson's tone was softer and he returned Nick's smile. "You gonna fuck me then, or what?"

"Well, excuse me for taking it slowly, Mr Impatient." Nick drew back and thrust in.

"Fuck!" Jackson groaned, but it sounded like a good groan so Nick carried on.

He rocked into Jackson with a steady rhythm and soon they were both making sounds of pleasure. Luckily there was nobody to overhear them—except maybe the people in the flat below, but only if they really went for it.

Jackson started jerking himself off, and Nick watched as his hand moved faster and faster until it was a blur. "Fuck me harder," Jackson gasped. "Oh yeah, don't stop. Gonna come. Fuck, *Nick*...." He tensed as the first spurt of come splashed over his abs.

Nick had been so focused on making sure Jackson was having a good time that he hadn't realised how turned on he was, but the sight of Jackson coming all over himself and the sound of his moans pulled Nick over the edge too. He thrust in one last time and his whole body shook as pleasure tore through him, making the room fade out for a moment.

He collapsed into Jackson's arms and lay there until he'd got his breath back.

"Wow," he said.

"Yeah. That was pretty awesome." Jackson's voice was warm.

"Well yes... that too. But also, I'd forgotten what hard work topping is. I'm knackered."

Jackson chuckled. "It is pretty good exercise. But like any exercise, the more you do it, the easier it gets."

"Well I'd better try and get plenty of practice in then, because my topping muscles are clearly a bit feeble."

"I volunteer to help with that training."

"I should hope so. Seeing as you're my boyfriend." Nick raised his head to look into Jackson's eyes. "You are my boyfriend now, right? For real?"

"Yeah. No more pretending. This is the real thing."

They smiled at each other, and warm happiness rose in Nick's chest, tightening his throat and making his eyes wet. What could be better than falling in love with your best friend and finding out he loved you back?

"I feel so lucky." His voice came out hoarse around the lump in his throat.

Jackson kissed him softly on the lips and whispered, "Me too."

EPILOGUE

Six months later

"OUCH!" Jackson exclaimed as he bashed his elbow. "I swear this tree's shrunk, or I've grown."

"You okay?"

"Yeah. I just knocked a bit of skin off my elbow. This was safer in the winter with more layers for protection."

"Yeah. It is a bit rough in places," Nick agreed.

"I'm nearly there.... *Oof!*" With a final surge of effort Jackson heaved himself up onto the wooden platform. "Okay," he called back to Nick. "I'm up."

"Well done." Nick scrambled up after Jackson.

"You could at least try and make it look like a challenge," Jackson said. "My ego is bruised now as well as my elbow."

"Sorry." Nick grinned. "But I've done this hundreds of times, remember? So I definitely have an advantage. Anyway. You were the one who insisted we climb up!"

"True." Jackson leant back to admire the view. It was very different from how he remembered it. With the morning sun already high in a cloudless blue sky, he was grateful for the partial shade of the leaves. Through the branches, the trees surrounding them were all decked in varying shades of green, many of them still in blossom. "It's so beautiful here."

"Isn't it?" Nick agreed, moving to sit beside him.

Jackson put his arm around Nick and they sat like that for a little while, soaking up the sounds and scents of the woods around them.

Despite the calm beauty of the setting, Jackson couldn't relax and enjoy it, because his heart was racing and his muscles were tight with anticipation. There was a reason he'd persuaded Nick they should visit his parents that weekend, and there was a reason he'd made Nick climb the Pirate Tree with him that morning.

It's going to be okay, he told himself.

But what if it isn't?

He couldn't bear to wait any longer, so he took a shaky breath and moved to kneel on the plank by Nick's feet. It was a little tight, but there was just enough space.

"What are you doing?" Nick asked, and then his face split into a knowing grin. "Oh I get it! That's why you wanted to come here. Awesome." He started to undo the button on his shorts. "I'm down for another round of tree blow jobs. Bring it on."

"No!" Jackson said quickly. "That's not... Nick. Stop!" He batted Nick's hand away from his fly.

"What's going on?" Nick's expression was a mix of disappointed and bewildered.

Jackson reached into his pocket and drew out a small black box. He opened the lid and held it out on his palm. The silver ring shone against dark green silk.

"Oh, shit!" Nick clapped his hand over his mouth, eyes wide as he stared wildly at the ring, then at Jackson, then back at the ring again.

Jackson had had a whole speech planned but it had flown out of his head at the unexpected turn this had taken. Instead, he simply asked the all-important question, "So.... Will you marry me?"

"Yes," Nick answered without hesitation. "Yes, definitely, totally." Then he gave an apologetic grin. "I'm sorry. I kind of ruined the moment, didn't I?"

Amusement and relief bubbled out of Jackson in a rich burst of laughter. "Not for me. This is perfect."

Nick took the ring and studied it. "Wow, this is lovely. Are those oak leaves etched on it?" He looked more closely. "And is that mistletoe as well?"

"Yes. Our first kiss was under the mistletoe in the kitchen, but our first *real* kiss was up the tree, so it seemed appropriate to have both."

"And our first blow job was in the tree too," Nick reminded him. "Do you want to put it on for me?"

Jackson slipped it on his finger and it fitted perfectly. "Do you like it?"

"I love it!" Nick turned his hand this way and that. "And I love why you chose that design. Can I get a similar one for you so we can be matching?"

"Of course."

"I'd been thinking about proposing too, but I was afraid it was too soon."

Jackson smiled. "We may have only been a couple for six months, but I reckoned all those years of friendship had to count for something, and I didn't see the point in waiting."

"Well, I'm glad you beat me to it." Nick leant forward and kissed him lightly on the lips. When he tried to draw back, Jackson slid a hand into his hair and deepened the kiss. His other hand found Nick's thigh and he let it drift towards Nick's crotch until he found the bulge of his dick. Breaking the kiss, he said, "You can get it out now if you want?"

Nick grinned, bright eyed and flushed. "Hell yes, I want! Can I suck yours after too?"

"Absolutely."

THEY WALKED BACK through the woods hand in hand. As they approached the gate to the garden, Nick said, "Can I tell them?"

"About us getting engaged?"

"What else? I wasn't planning on telling them about the blow jobs."

Jackson laughed. "Probably for the best. And yes, of course. You're wearing the ring, so they might notice anyway."

They'd spent enough time with Nick's parents since Christmas for Jackson to be fairly sure they'd be happy about this development, but even so, there were jitters in his stomach as they walked through the garden.

Thankfully both Nick's parents were in the kitchen, and Jackson didn't have to wait any longer because Nick burst through the door saying, "Mum, Dad... there's something I need to tell you!"

They both turned, attention caught by his excitement.

Nick held up his hand, and the silver metal glinted where the light caught it.

"Oh!" Sue gasped, one hand coming to her heart.

"Jackson asked me to marry him." Nick beamed. "And I said yes—obviously."

"That's wonderful news," Reg said with a huge smile. "Congratulations, both of you!" He abandoned his crossword and got up to shake Jackson's hand, and then Nick's—but Nick pulled him into a hug instead.

"Yes, congratulations!" Sue gave them both hugs and kisses. "What lovely news. So how did you do it, Jackson. Did you go down on one knee?"

"Technically I think it was both knees," Jackson said.

"He proposed to me in the Pirate Tree," Nick explained. "So space was a bit tight."

"Let me see the ring?" Sue took Nick's hand. "Oh, Jackson. It's beautiful! I love the leaf design. What's the significance?"

"Well... our first proper kiss was under some mistletoe in the Pirate Tree," Jackson said. He saw the beginning of a smirk on Nick's face, so he shot him a warning glare. "Hence the oak leaves as well as the mistletoe, and that's why I took him back there to propose."

"Your first kiss?" Sue's brows drew down in confusion. "But how can that be? Christmas was the first time you visited here and you were already together then."

Shit. Much too late, Jackson realised his mistake. "Um...." He looked desperately at Nick for support.

Nick's expression flitted through shock, to mild panic, and quickly settled on resignation. He sighed and rolled his eyes. "Nice one, Jackson. You've just totally blown our cover on Operation Fake Relationship. But I guess now at least we can use it in our wedding speeches, because it will be good fodder for that. Bags I get to tell it though, because it was my idea."

"Nick. What *are* you talking about?" Reg asked.

"Well." Nick gave a nervous laugh. "Okay, um. Funny story...."

ABOUT THE AUTHOR

Jay lives just outside Bristol in the West of England. He comes from a family of writers, but always used to believe that the gene for fiction writing had passed him by. He spent years only ever writing emails, articles, or website content.
One day, Jay decided to try and write a short story—just to see if he could—and found it rather addictive. He hasn't stopped writing since.

www.jaynorthcote.com
Twitter: @Jay_Northcote
Facebook: Jay Northcote Fiction

MORE FROM JAY NORTHCOTE

The Rainbow Place Series

Rainbow Place - Rainbow Place #1
Safe Place - Rainbow Place #2
Better Place - Rainbow Place #3
Mud & Lace - Rainbow Place #4
Happy Place - Rainbow Place #5

The Housemates Series

Helping Hand – Housemates #1
Like a Lover – Housemates #2
Practice Makes Perfect – Housemates #3
Watching and Wanting – Housemates #4
Starting from Scratch – Housemates #5
Pretty in Pink – Housemates #6

Novels and Novellas

Nothing Serious
Nothing Special
Nothing Ventured
Not Just Friends
Passing Through
The Little Things
The Dating Game – Owen & Nathan #1
The Marrying Kind – Owen & Nathan #2
The Law of Attraction
Imperfect Harmony
Into You
Cold Feet
What Happens at Christmas
A Family for Christmas
Secret Santa
Stuck With You
Summer Heat
Tops Down Bottoms Up
The Half Wolf
Second Chance
Where Love Grows
A Boyfriend for Christmas